DUE TO TECHNICAL DIFFICULTIES . . .

"So I guess there's no way out of this thing," Billy the Kid said.

Garrett shook his head. "Not unless you want to surrender peaceable and come back with me."

Billy's hand flashed to the Colt, but to his horrified surprise he wasn't fast enough. There was a bang, a puff of smoke, and he was thrown back onto the hot, red dirt of the street. This wasn't supposed to be happening. He was supposed to kill Garrett and then go back to the cantina for a final fling. He wasn't supposed to die.

He was suddenly on his feet again. "So I guess there's no way out of this thing."

"Not unless you want to surrender peaceable and come back with me."

Billy's hand flashed to the Colt, but he wasn't fast enough . . .

By Mick Farren
Published by Ballantine Books:

THE ARMAGEDDON CRAZY
THE FEELIES
THE LAST STAND OF THE DNA COWBOYS
THE LONG ORBIT
MARS—THE RED PLANET
THEIR MASTER'S WAR

THE
FEELIES

Mick Farren

A Del Rey Book
BALLANTINE BOOKS • NEW YORK

This book is dedicated to the memory of the late Michael Dempsey who demonstrated that, on a bad night, it can take more than one Irishman to screw in a light bulb.

IT WAS THE THIRD TIME THAT JOHN Wilson Heffer had taken a feelie. The previous times, he had only been able to afford a twelve-hour quickie, but since his promotion and the raise that had gone with it, he had found himself in the position, subject to a certain adjustment in his spending habits, to splurge on the whole weekend package. He had been living out the life of Billy the Kid for the past twenty-eight hours and still had another twenty to go, culminating in the famous gunfight with Pat Garrett. Of course, history had been somewhat rearranged for the purpose of the feelie. In this version Billy survived and Garrett was ceremoniously carted off to Boot Hill by weeping whores and the mariachi band from the cantina. The idea of a feelie in which the subject died was unthinkable to Heffer. Only the most perverse entertained the desire to go through the experience of simulated death, and although there were rumors that it did circulate on the underground market, snuff software was extremely illegal.

Even with his raise and his scrimping, Heffer might not have been able to come up with the money for forty-eight hours in the Billy the Kid experience if it hadn't been on the weekend discount list. In the last couple of years, western adventures had fallen from favor, and very few new ones were being made at all. Public taste had changed, and the majority now went for psychedelic space fantasy, the incredibly violent Supersoldier series, and, of course, the fifty-seven hundred varieties of sex scenario that were in the catalog in a section all to themselves. John Wilson Heffer was a traditionalist. He prided

1

himself that he had no time for trends and fads. He still
liked the hot sun and the cool dark saloons and the wide-
open spaces of the Old West. That wasn't to say that the
western fantasies weren't without their share of both sex
and violence. In the past twenty-eight hours, he had killed
six men, made love to four women, two of them at the
same time, drunk three bottles of whiskey, and won four
hundred dollars in gold from three pistoleers and a dude
in a fancy vest who had just come in off the stage. Unfortunately, he'd had to shoot two of the pistoleers in
order to walk away with his winnings. Of course, there
was considerable telescoping in feelie fantasy. He was
under no illusion that the real Billy the Kid had ever
accomplished so much in a single day. Heffer had no
objection to that. He wasn't offended that a certain plau-
sibility was sacrificed to cost effectiveness and customer
satisfaction. All in all, he was fairly satisfied with the
subjective sensation that he was the baddest desperado in
all of Lincoln County.

He was also aware, however, that hardly anything was
perfect. In this case, it was the software. There was a
serious imbalance in the sensory inputs. The audio was
normal enough; but the olfactory and the tactile were
way up, while the visual was right down, indistinct and
muddy. The daytime on the streets was all glare and
shimmer, while the nights in the saloons were dark, out
of focus Rembrandts where he had to rely on impression
rather than actual sight.

No matter how deeply he went into the fantasy, a small,
objective part of his mind always remained apart from
the adopted identity. It simply watched and observed. It
was that part of him that was determined that he should
say something once the experience was over. The feelie
really wasn't good enough. Sure, he was enjoying himself, but that was hardly the point. It was a matter of
principle. Once they'd laid you out in the plastic cabinet
that was just a little too much like a coffin, connected

the electrodes, and put you under, it was too late. You couldn't come out of the indream to complain about the software quality. All that should have been checked out up front. The discount notwithstanding, he had paid a small fortune for this weekend, and he wasn't about to tolerate a poor visual and overpowering smells. He was going to demand a refund.

It had been the smells that had hit him first. His own smell was less than pleasant: a mixture of acrid sweat, old leather, gun oil, and hot metal. The catalog had neglected to mention that Billy the Kid appeared to bathe on something like an annual basis and only shaved maybe once a week. That posed a bit of a problem for the normally fastidious Heffer. He had experienced nothing like this when he had spent twelve hours as Bat Masterson. Masterson had been extremely clean and had changed his shirt no less than three times in the course of the fantasy. Walking into the cantina had been the worst. As he had come through the batwing doors, the wave of stale beer, rank cigar smoke, and the sweat of men as filthy as himself had all but knocked him off his feet. He had been quite unable to enjoy the way the place had fallen silent and the piano player had stopped playing. The unwashed smell of the mexicali whores, which they couldn't disguise even with liberal amounts of cheap perfume, had all but made him gag.

The overloaded tactile inputs, on the other hand, were something else again. They gave everything a strange edge that, although uncomfortable at times, could also be extremely exhilarating. During the gunfights, when the Colt Peacemaker—an accurate replica of the Kid's own custom-made weapon, the one with the unusual curved, eagle-beak handle—bucked in his hand, the sensation made him feel close to godlike. And the women. In that area, he had no complaints about the tactile overload. Heffer's therapist had told him on a number of occasions that he was too much of a prude to truly enjoy

himself, but in this instance, he had broken out and gone
mindlessly wild. When he climbed the stairs with a sa-
loon girl on each arm, he was moved to a previously
unattainable level of physical delight. They were like a
pair of bright-eyed, golden-skinned animals, sinuous and
sensual, with swirling manes of jet-black hair. They gig-
gled and they did things to him, and he, as Billy the Kid,
accepted it as his due tribute. Their mouths, their hands,
the smooth heat of their inner thighs working on him in
turns and together, had taken him to places that he had
never been before. He even managed to lose himself so
completely that he had forgotten about their lack of personal hygiene and his own fear of disease. What the hell,
he had told himself. You can't catch a retrovirus from an
electronically induced illusion no matter how bad she
might smell.

Billy the Kid/Heffer drank and whored through the long
afternoon. In a feelie, the fictional principal never slept,
and there were no bad aftereffects. The recipient, on the
other hand, technically slept all the time; although his or
her brain was racing, the body was under the impression
that it was enjoying deep, untroubled REM sleep. Garrett
was coming at sunset, and the whole town knew it. A
hot, lazy tension was building. Little kids played in the
street, antagonizing scorpions with burning twigs.
Tongue-lolling dogs stretched out flat in patches of shade
under the wooden sidewalk. Someone somewhere was
playing a guitar, a mournful Spanish dirge in a minor
key, all about love, betrayal, and murder. "The Flowers
of Evil." Heffer found that he could understand the lyrics
even though he normally couldn't speak a word of Spanish. Inside the cantina, the men of the town sat with their
tequila and their slices of lime and watched him. He was
the marked one. He was the one who might be dead before the darkness gathered. They watched him for any
slip, a word or a look, a shake of the hand, anything that
might be a sign of weakness or fear. Billy the Kid/Heffer

laughed at them. He had the wild confidence of the young, reckless, and drunk. Pat Garrett, badge or no badge, wasn't going to be a problem.

Finally, he was out on the street. The sun was dipping to the horizon against a blood-red sky. He positioned himself with his back to the blaze of the sunset. His shadow stretched out black in front of him, almost twenty feet long, straight down the center of the street. Garrett would be coming in from the east with the sun in his eyes. Billy/Heffer had the edge. His hands curled and uncurled, eager to grab the pistol in his belt, squeeze the trigger, and feel it kick in his hand. When Garrett was dead, he was going back to the cantina. Very soon, his time in the feelie would be up, and he wanted one more bottle and one more woman before he returned to the real workaday, Monday morning world of John Wilson Heffer. It would be a long time before he could afford another weekend contract.

Garrett was coming—the setting sun glinted on the pearl-handled six shooters in the crossdraw rig and the Winchester rifle he was holding at his side. Billy/Heffer laughingly called out a greeting.

"So how you doing, Pat? It's been a while since you were down in these parts."

"I've come to take you back to Santa Fe for trial, Billy."

"I really don't be planning to go anywhere, Pat. I kind of like it here."

"I don't want to be having to kill you, Billy."

"Hell, Pat, you been acting plain damn mean since you started working for the Santa Fe Ring. I thought you and me were supposed to be friends."

"The country's changing, Billy, and friendships have gotta change along with it."

"So I guess there's no way out of this thing."

Garrett shook his head. "Not unless you want to surrender peaceable and come back with me."

"You know I can't do that."

"Then I don't see no way out. We better get to it."

Without another word, Billy/Heffer's hand flashed to the Colt, but to his horrified surprise he wasn't fast enough. The rifle was in Garrett's hand before his own pistol was even clear of its holster. There was a bang, a puff of smoke, and, immediately afterward, a searing, burning pain in his chest that was made doubly bad by the overloaded tactile input. He was thrown back onto the hot, red dirt of the street. This wasn't supposed to be happening. He was supposed to kill Garrett and then go back to the cantina for a final fling. He wasn't supposed to die. Feelies didn't do things like this.

He was suddenly on his feet again.

"So I guess there's no way out of this thing."

"Not unless you want to surrender peaceable and come back with me."

"You know I can't do that."

"Then I don't see no way out. We'd better get to it."

Without another word, Billy/Heffer's hand flashed to the Colt, but he wasn't fast enough. The rifle was in Garrett's hand before his own pistol was even clear of its holster. There was a bang, a puff of smoke, and, immediately afterward, a searing, burning pain in his chest. He was thrown back onto the hot, red dirt of the street. This wasn't supposed to be happening. The software was crashing. It was stuck in some kind of loop. Someone had to be monitoring this. They had to notice that something was wrong and get him out. He couldn't just be left like this.

"So I guess there's no way out of this thing."

"Not unless you want to surrender peaceable and come back with me."

"You know I can't do that."

"Then I don't see no way out. We'd better get to it."

Without another word, Billy/Heffer's hand flashed to the Colt, but he wasn't fast enough. The rifle was in

Garrett's hand before his own pistol was even clear of its holster. There was a bang, a puff of smoke, and, immediately afterward, a searing, burning pain in his chest. He was thrown back into the hot, red dirt of the street. This wasn't supposed to be happening. This wasn't just a glitch—this was a major malfunction. The software was seriously screwing up, and he was trapped inside it, going around and around and having an agonizingly painful bullet smash into his chest each time the cycle was completed. The worst part was that he was totally helpless. His guts were wrenching, already anticipating the next bullet from the Winchester. The detached part of his mind, the piece of his consciousness that would have no part of the Billy the Kid personality was well on the way to screaming panic. Someone had to be monitoring this. They had to get him out. He couldn't take being shot one more time.

"So I guess there's no way out of this thing."

"Not unless you want to surrender peaceable and come back with me."

His detached mind was screaming: For God's sake! Anybody! Somebody! Get me out of here!

IT WAS AN AVERAGE DAY IN 5066 SECtion of the vault. The stiffs lay in neat rows in their plastic cases. The red-power lights glowed unwinkingly on the control pacs at the foot of each case. A continuous high-pitched hum, on the very limits of normal hearing, was about the only sound. Sam sat on the concrete floor with his back resting against a row of cases. He was turning over a tamperproof twenty flatpack of Serenax in his pudgy fingers. He'd had three already and he felt a little woozy, but he knew that, sooner or later, he would crack open the new pack. Five years earlier, Serenax had been available by prescription only. Now it was sold over the counter. There were even vending machines on the subway. Serenax: "Dangerous to Exceed the Recommended Dose." Sam exceeded the recommended dose on a daily basis. Sam was a squat, overweight figure in drab tan overalls. In truth, he only appeared squat. If he straightened up, he was well over six feet tall. The trouble was that Sam rarely straightened up. He was perpetually stooped and sagging.

Ralph was at the far end of the same row, going through the motions of sweeping. There was really nothing to sweep. The vault was virtually dust free. It was that point in the day when he couldn't stand being near the other two. Ralph was the complete opposite of Sam. Where Sam was gross and slothful, Ralph was thin and frenetic. He was a good three inches shorter than Sam. He had the features of a nervous but cunning rodent. His eyes constantly darted from spot to spot, as though expecting some sort of threat. A nerve twitched just below his left cheekbone. It only stopped when he was drunk.

Artie had vanished somewhere, probably on some devious errand of his own. Artie was always vanishing. It was his way. He made up the final third of the maintenance and monitor crew of 5066 section. Artie was lucky that they had lax management and a good union.

Sam reluctantly put the still unopened flatpack in the pocket of his overalls and looked around. "Hey, Ralph."

Ralph pretended not to hear. He went on with his sweeping.

"Hey, Ralph."

Ralph realized that if he ignored Sam any longer, the dummy would probably get up and come lurching over. He stopped sweeping. The muscles in his shoulders and neck felt bunched and tense. "What's the matter, Sam?"

"Where do you think Artie's got to?"

"How should I know where Artie's got to?"

"He's been gone a long time."

"Who knows where Artie goes to?"

"Do you think—"

Ralph cut Sam off. "Sam."

"Yes, Ralph?"

Ralph felt a bad need for a drink. "Sam."

"Yes, Ralph."

"Will you do something for me?"

"Sure, Ralph."

"Will you shut the fuck up?"

"I was only—"

"Shut up, Sam."

Ralph could feel an edge creeping into his voice. He was starting to loose control. Sam recognized the change in tone, and his hand moved defensively toward the Serenax in his pocket.

"Sure, Ralph."

Sam seemed to slump a little.

Ralph picked up his broom and moved down two more rows of cabinets. He needed to get farther away from Sam. He also had a bottle stashed along there. He put down his broom and reached between two of the plastic cases. Resting on a pipe was a bottle of cheap Japanese Scotch. Ralph held it up. It was just short of half full. Ralph grinned to himself. He must be in a fairly optimistic mood, otherwise he'd be looking at the bottle as more than half empty.

Ralph glanced into the nearest case. The occupant was an overweight, self-satisfied, middle-aged male. Plastic tubes went up each nostril, and a tangle of thin, multicolored wires were attached to shaved parts of his head. Ralph knew from experience that other tubes and wires were hooked into the stiff's torso, but these were hidden by the green plastic body bag that covered everything but its head.

The stiff's name was stenciled on the body bag. Morton Jonas Berkowitz. It was followed by a serial number. Ralph shrugged. It was as good as any other. He hunkered down on the floor and rested his back against the cabinet. He took a long pull on the bottle. The sudden explosion of warmth in his gut was intensely satisfying, so satisfying that it killed the feeling of self-disgust that usually followed him around. Ralph was aware that booze was well on its way to being all that he lived for.

It was obvious that the place was getting to him. He looked around at 5066 section of the vaults. Not that it was different from any other section. It was gray. The same deathly gray quiet was broken only by the continuous electric hum. There were the same flat gray concrete walls, gray roof, and solid gray supporting pillars. The vault was lit by cold neon lights, spaced so far apart that it was a place of almost sinister, antiseptic gloom. The shadows went on as far as the eye could see. If you worked in the vault you could start to think it went on forever.

Ralph took another drink. The disgust was starting to come back. Even the goddamn job was a farce. There was no need for human operators in the vaults. The whole place was run automatically off the computer bank.

"Operators!"

Even the word was a joke. They weren't operators. They were just fucking unemployables, stuck in the vault, sitting around, drinking, taking drugs, and maybe doing a spot of sweeping. They were only kept there by the union agreements.

"Motherfuckers."

Ralph slammed his fist into the control pac of the nearest cabinet. The red light didn't even blink. The red lights were the only warm color in the entire place. The Krupp DR.40 control pacs were just about indestructible. Ralph knew that he didn't have a dog's chance of ever getting on a feelie. You had to have a B+ or more even to hook in for a weekend. Ralph's credit card had an unmistakable D on it. The lifers, the ones he had to watch all day, were solid As. They were the fat bastards who had cashed in all their assets and retired to a world of total fantasy for the rest of their lives. The only chance that Ralph had to go that route was to win one of the big prizes on the TV quiz shows, and everyone knew the quiz shows were fixed.

Ralph felt a helpless, impotent anger welling up inside him. He felt like hurling the bottle across the vault. He restrained himself. There was still about three inches of Scotch in the bottle.

He climbed unsteadily to his feet and lurched down the row of cabinets. He had to make an effort to focus his eyes. A red light had gone out and the plastic cover on the case was misted over on the inside. It was coated with a kind of dirty, off-white condensation.

"Jesus Christ!"

Ralph tried to pull himself together. The booze made it difficult. "Sam?"

Sam didn't move. The fat figure was apparently asleep.

Ralph yelled louder. "Sam!"

Sam lifted his head. "Huh?"

"Get on your feet, will you? We've got a malfunction over here."

Sam's small eyes blinked rapidly. "A malfunction?"

Sam was obviously too tranquil to be able to take much in.

"Just get on your feet, will you?"

"Huh?"

"Christ, Sam! Just get up, you cretin."

While Sam struggled to get to his feet, Ralph opened the inspection cover on the control pac. He located the emergency release button and pressed it. The cabinet seals popped and the cover swung slowly open. Ralph almost gagged at the stench that emerged from inside. He grabbed the cover and slammed it shut.

"Sam! Will you get the hell over here?"

"I'm coming, Ralph, I'm coming."

The shock had cleared Ralph's head a little. He went to the nearest pillar with a phone point on it. He picked up the white wall phone and waited. After a minute or so, a bored voice came down the line.

"Yeah?"

"This is 5066, we've got a malfunction down here."

"Shit." The voice sounded annoyed. "Is the stiff dead?"

"It sure smelled dead."

"You cracked open the cabinet?"

"Right."

"Okay, wait a minute." There was a pause while the voice seemed to be talking to someone else. "Listen, 5066 is a lifer section, yeah?"

"Yeah."

"Yeah, okay."

There was another pause. Finally the voice came back. "Okay, 5066, stay where you are and we'll get someone down there to deal with it."

The voice sounded bored again. Ralph hung up. Sam was staring glumly at the misted-over cover of the cabinet.

"We don't get many of these."

"For Christ's sake, don't touch anything. It stinks to high heaven under that cover."

The two of them stood by the cabinet. Ralph hitched his thumbs in the back pockets of his overalls.

"Ain't nothing we can do but wait, I guess."

Sam grunted. "Ain't nothing else we ever do but wait."

Ralph sniffed. "That's a fact."

Sam absently scratched his armpit. "Sometimes I wonder what we're waiting for."

It was a good fifteen minutes before they saw the white golf cart coming almost silently down the avenue between the cabinets. It halted with a metallic click. Two men climbed out. They were uniformly clean shaven, healthy, fresh-faced, and scrubbed. They both had the same neat blond crewcuts. Their starched white intern suits contrasted sharply with Ralph's and Sam's stained tan overalls.

They got out of the cart with an air of assured efficiency.

"Okay, what we got here? A malfunctioning stiff, right?"

Ralph stuffed his hands deep in his pockets. "Right."

"Dead?"

"Seems that way."

The clean-cut young men moved toward the cabinet.

"We'll take care of this now."

One of them flipped open the cover of the control pac. Ralph walked in a small circle, hands still in his pockets.

"I wouldn't—"

He was stopped briskly. "It's okay. I told you we're taking care of things now."

"Suit yourself."

The other pressed the emergency release. Both the fresh-faced young men doubled up as the stench hit them. Ralph already had a rag pressed to his face. Sam didn't appear to notice.

Ralph walked over to the cabinet and banged down the lid. "I warned you."

The scrubbed young men gradually regained their composure.

"How the hell long has that stiff been dead?"

Ralph shrugged. "How the hell should I know?"

"You work in this section."

"So?"

"You should have seen the light had gone out."

"I sent for you, didn't I?"

"That was all of half an hour ago."

Ralph pulled his hands out of his pockets. "What exactly are you trying to say?"

"Jesus Christ, man, that stiff's been dead for a week. How come you didn't notice until half an hour ago?"

Ralph shrugged again.

"You haven't even walked down this row for a week."

"Sure I've walked down this row. I stash my goddamn—" Ralph realized he had gone too far. The clean-cut young men's eyebrows shot up. "Nothing."

One of the crewcut young men started in again. "We're going to report this whole thing, make no mistake about that."

The other one grabbed him by the arm. "Come on, Craig. We don't have time to argue about all this."

Ralph grinned. "He's right . . . Craig. How come your monitor system didn't pick up the fact that this stiff was dead?"

Craig scowled. "Okay, okay, we don't have time to argue about it."

"Let's get down to it."

The scrubbed young men took two gas masks out of a compartment in the golf cart. Craig waved in the direction of Ralph and Sam.

"You guys better get back out of the way."

"Yeah, sure."

Ralph wandered off. Sam followed him. The two crewcut young men put on their gas masks and took a heavy-duty body bag out of another compartment in the golf cart. They went to work on the corpse. Their last move was to drag out an industrial aerosol and start spraying the whole area. Ralph and Sam came walking back as the scrubbed young men were removing their gas masks.

"You taken care of it, then?"

"Yeah. Everything's taken care of."

"I guess you'll be putting a new stiff in there soon?"

"Yeah, pretty soon."

Ralph pointed at the body bag. "You'll have to break the bad news to that one's next of kin, I expect."

The crewcut young men dumped the body bag in the back of the golf cart. They quickly climbed inside.

"Uh, yeah. That's right. We'll be breaking the bad news."

As they rolled away, Ralph went and picked up his bottle. He grinned after them. "Yeah. Damn right you will."

AS TRUMBLE WALKED UP TO THE GLASS doors, they slid open for him. Inside the carpet was thick, the lighting soft, and the air-conditioning comfortingly cool. The office was furnished in deep orange and rich browns. Gold gleamed in low-key satisfaction. Everything seemed designed to put Trumble at his ease. Whoever had planned it all had succeeded in the seemingly impossible task of combining the ambience of a bank with that of a massage parlor.

A receptionist approached him. She was wearing an orange dress, one of that summer's exotiques. It was long at the back but swept up in a long inverted V clear up to a pair of matching panties. The slit in the skirt was echoed by the deep V in the neckline that plunged between the girl's handsome breasts to end somewhere close to her waist.

Her smile was as fashionable and as synthetic as her outfit. Her teeth were frighteningly perfect.

"Can I help you, sir?"

Trumble couldn't take his eyes off her perfect teeth. He could feel himself starting to sweat.

"Uh, yes."

The girl waited. She regarded him with an immaculate blend of coolness and expectant interest. Combined Media only employed the best.

Trumble pulled himself together. "I'd like to reserve some feelie time."

The girl was gently remonstrative. "We prefer to talk about it as Integrated Entertainment."

Trumble tried to smile. "That's quite a mouthful."

"IE for short."

"Okay then, I'd like to book some IE time."

The girl's smile went into full gear. "That's what we're here for, sir." She motioned to a neat row of desks that ran down the far side of the office. "If you go and talk to Wendy at desk twenty-nine, I'm sure she can take care of everything for you."

Trumble thanked her and plowed his way across the expanse of carpet. The girl at desk twenty-nine was dressed identically to the receptionist. The flawless smile came from the same mold, as did the equally flawless hair and figure. On the desk in front of her was a small sign that read "Hi—I'm Wendy."

"Hi, Wendy."

"Won't you take a seat, Mr. . . ."

"Trumble."

"Hi, Mr. Trumble. Please take a seat."

Trumble lowered himself into the offered chair.

Wendy's smile continued to radiate helpfulness. "What can I do for you, Mr. Trumble?"

"I'd like to book some fe—uh, IE time, if I may."

The girl nodded approvingly. "I'm sure I can work out something for you. How long a hook-up were you thinking of?"

"Uh . . . I thought I'd have forty-eight hours, a weekend, you know."

"I'm sure it'll be a weekend you won't forget. When did you want to make the hook-up?"

"The weekend after next. That's what I was thinking of."

"One moment, Mr. Trumble."

Wendy turned to a discreetly positioned computer console and entered a series of figures. After a short pause, the answer flashed up on a tiny screen recessed in the desktop.

"I think that'll be okay. How did you intend to pay, Mr. Trumble?"

Trumble fumbled for his wallet. "By card, the usual way."

"Could I see your card for a moment, please?"

Trumble pulled out his credit card and passed it across the desk. The girl's smile dimmed a couple of points. She turned the card over in her fingers. The impeccable fingernails clicked softly on the plastic. She looked at Trumble more in sorrow than in anger.

"I see your rating is C−, Mr. Trumble."

Trumble knew he was sweating. "Yes, that's right."

"Well, Mr. Trumble, you must realize that the kind of weekend you're talking about isn't exactly . . . inexpensive."

Trumble cut in hastily. "Yes, yes. I've looked at the prices. I know all about them." He hesitated. "I've been saving up, you see. This weekend means a lot to me. I've been saving for a long time."

Wendy turned up her smile. "I see. I'll have to check on that before I can make your reservation."

Trumble nodded swiftly. "Yes, yes, that's all right. I don't mind."

Wendy dropped the card into the console. After another short wait, something flashed up on the screen. Trumble couldn't read it upside down, but Wendy's smile became even more radiant.

"You have been saving, haven't you, Mr. Trumble?"

Trumble blushed. "I've been looking forward to this weekend for quite a while."

"All we have to do now is pick the particular experience you have in mind."

Trumble began to redden again. "I . . . er."

"Would you like to look through our listings of possible options, Mr. Trumble?"

Wendy offered him a thick spiral-bound booklet with a plastic cover. Trumble could feel sweat running down from his armpits. He turned over pages at random. His thumbs and fingers felt twice their normal thickness. He glanced up. Wendy was watching him with a knowing, conspiratorial smile.

"I think we already know the experience we want, don't we, Mr. Trumble?"

Trumble's tongue was threatening to choke him. "I . . ."

"Come now, Mr. Trumble, you don't have to be embarrassed. You won't shock me. I won't laugh at you."

"I don't . . ."

"I'm here to help you, Mr. Trumble."

Trumble knew it was now or never. If he didn't do it now, he would change his mind and blow his savings on some experience he didn't even want. It all came blurting out in a stammering rush.

"I—I want to be the Marquis de Sade."

Without a word or the slightest flicker of expression, Wendy started tapping out yet another set of figures. Trumble sat frozen, amazed that he had actually done it. Wendy punched up his reservation. A receipt and a slip with date and time on it were printed out of the machine. Wendy took a multicolored folder from the desk and stapled them into it. She handed it to Trumble with a cool, even look.

"I'm sure it will be a very rewarding weekend, Mr. Trumble."

WANDA-JEAN BECAME CONSCIOUS. THE first thing she realized was that it was a mistake. She had a pain in her head that stretched all the way down the back of her neck. Her mouth was full of evil-tasting, contaminated cotton waste, and she felt sick to her stomach.

It was yet another morning after a night on the circuit of boom-boom bars along 3d Street.

With almost independent life, her left hand crawled across the sheet toward the far side of the bed. There was nobody there. The bastard had gone. Her memories of getting home the night before were hazy. She could just about remember that he had short-cropped, dark hair and broad shoulders. She suspected that she had disliked him from the start.

She knew they had come back to her flat, fallen into bed, and had sex. After that she must have passed out. Some time between her passing out and the morning, he must have gotten up, dressed, and crept away. He probably had a wife or a girlfriend stashed away somewhere.

Wanda-Jean's right hand groped at the table beside the bed. She shook a cigarette out of a nearly empty pack. She rolled over on her side and stuck it in her mouth. She paused for nearly half a minute and then lit it.

Almost immediately she started to cough. Wanda-Jean wasn't quite able to handle doing two things at once. Coughing and keeping a grip on her stomach was more than she could manage. She made it to the bathroom just in time.

Afterward Wanda-Jean walked unsteadily into the

kitchen area. Throwing up had helped her hangover, but the comedown from the three decks of Blind Tiger she had bought from that Korean hustler when she had been drunk had moved into its place. She found a nearly clean glass and filled it from the water cooler, but then a bad fit of the trembles hit her and she had to put the glass down quickly. She leaned on the cooler, half doubled over, praying that they would go away.

The trembles subsided after a couple of minutes, and Wanda-Jean tentatively straightened up. Generally she tried to avoid taking drugs first thing in the morning, but she was going to have to make an exception. Even if she called in sick, she would need something just to see her back to bed.

An unpleasant thought suddenly struck her. Maybe the bastard had stolen her drugs. Maybe he had even glommed her smartcard. Pain forgotten, she fled in panic to the bedroom. Her bag lay among the discarded clothes. She wrenched it open and tipped the contents onto the bed. To her relief, both her smartcard and her enamel pill box with the picture of a dragon on it were among the debris. With a sigh, she sat down on the bed. She opened the box. There was half a deck of Tiger still wrapped in its original tinfoil, two Serenax, an octagon, and a valium. Just seeing that she still had the pills made her feel better.

Wanda-Jean knew she had to put some clothes on. She certainly didn't feel like roaming around nude all day. Putting on clothes meant she had to make up her mind whether to go to work or not that day. The pills were making her feel a good deal better. Not better enough, though, to smile brightly at dumb, pussy-mouthed customers all day. She decided to skip work.

She returned to the bedroom in search of a sweatshirt and a pair of pants. A close look at the discarded clothes from the night before stopped her dead.

''Motherfucker.''

She grabbed the black satin dress off the floor and held it up. It was ripped all down its length.

"Dirty bastard."

Wanda-Jean's rage spilled over, and she hurled the dress into a corner. The dress had cost her an arm and a leg. She must have gone to work for three solid days to get that dress, and the bastard ripped it pulling it off her. She'd only worn it twice. It was strictly a boom-boom room number, with the skirt cut away up to her crotch and the deep V neck that showed off her tits. Her fury increased when she noticed that the matching satin briefs were also torn.

"I'd like to castrate that son of a bitch."

She sat down on the bed, hugged her anger to herself, and cursed silently and steadily.

The pills didn't let her stay mad for very long. After a while she stood up and looked at her body in the full-length bedroom mirror.

Wanda-Jean liked her body. According to the magazines and movies, she had a good body. She always showed a high score in the kind of Know Your Attraction Count questionnaires on the sex and beauty shows. To her eyes, her legs were too long and her shoulders too broad, but none of the men she knew had ever done anything but pay her compliments.

Although it was a little confusing, Wanda-Jean was satisfied with her body. She did, however, suspect that if it was really first class, she would have gotten further in the world. The only thing that worried her about it was that one day it would start to fail. It would wrinkle, the breasts would sag, and it would no longer have the effect on men that it had right now. Wanda-Jean liked having an effect on men.

She wasn't as happy about her face. She had always wanted one of those aloof, perfectly proportioned faces like May Marsh who played the nurse in "Penal Colony" on Channel 80. Compared with May Marsh, Wanda-

Jean's nose was too long and her mouth too wide. Wanda-Jean spent a lot of time and money trying to hide these defects. In moments of depression she managed to convince herself they were her main stumbling blocks. If she got really low, words like *cheap* and *common* sprang to mind.

She turned slowly around, craning her neck to look at as much of herself as she could. Then she did it again. She noted that she carried some legacies from the previous night in the form of bruises and scratches. On another level, she looked at the marks with a certain degree of satisfaction. What was the point of spending the night with a guy if you didn't have a few bruises to show for it? She would still kick the bastard in the nuts, though, if she ever met him again and recognized him.

With the bout of narcissism over, Wanda-Jean became busy and businesslike. She stuffed her party clothes into the closet and pulled out a red sweatshirt and a pair of white jeans. The sweatshirt had the badge of a well-known Brazilian university on the front. Wanda-Jean had never been near a university, or Brazil, for that matter, but she thought it gave her class. She laid the things on the bed and went to take her shower.

By the time she was dressed and dry, Wanda-Jean was humming to herself. After breakfast, over her second cup of coffee, she began to think what she would do with the day. She picked up the phone to see if any messages had been left. There was nothing except some all-subscriber commercials.

She began to feel depressed. The pills were starting to wear off. Wanda-Jean felt lonely and unloved. That was the trouble with living on the twenty-fifth floor of a faceless, downtown security block. You were always so goddamn alone. It seemed as though she only met people in order to have a bit of quick sex. Even then, they ran out in the middle of the night.

Wanda-Jean picked up her pill box again. It was too

early to take the half deck. Instead she dug out a packet of chewing gum and started unwrapping it, then stopped. Maybe something had come for her in the mail.

She went to the door of the apartment and opened the mailbox. There were two circulars, a reminder on an unpaid bill, and a long white envelope. Wanda-Jean picked up the envelope. It was very expensive paper, not like the usual letters she received.

She turned it over. It was correctly addressed. In the top right-hand corner was the logo of the National Cable Corporation. Why should NCC want to write to her?

For a moment a nasty thought flashed in her mind. She'd forgotten to pay for the TV. She was going to be cut off. That couldn't be true, though. She'd taken care of the cable payment only a few days earlier. And anyway, they didn't send final demands in expensive envelopes.

Wanda-Jean tore it open. Inside was a white, engraved card. Wanda-Jean looked at the print in disbelief. Almost in a trance she walked back into the kitchen and sat down.

It didn't seem possible. They had only filled in the applications as a joke. She and her friends Shirley and June had been drunk one night. She had never imagined that it would go any further.

She read the words for the tenth time.

You are invited to audition as a contestant on the NCC game production—*WILDEST DREAMS.*
For further details call 9000-9000 during normal office hours. This application is only valid until November 2.

November 2 was only two days away. Wanda-Jean thoughtfully put a stick of gum in her mouth and picked up the phone. Carefully she dialed 9000-0000.

"THE GAME SHOWS?"

Ralph looked at Sam in contempt. "You don't believe in the fucking game shows, do you?"

Sam looked at him blankly. "I was just saying that the game shows are the only way the likes of you and me are going to ever get to be lifers."

Ralph snapped around at him. "You think you and me are ever going to get on 'Wildest Dreams' or 'Lifetime Chance'?"

"Why not, Ralph? We got the same chance as everyone else."

"Bullshit."

"But why not, Ralph?"

Ralph's patience gave out. "Because the game shows are fucking fixed. That's why!"

Sam didn't answer. He looked glumly at the floor. Sam and Ralph sat side by side on the floor with their backs resting against the row of cases. They had given up all idea of even seeming to do any work. They just sat there, Sam with his Serenax and Ralph with his bottle.

"Why, Ralph?"

Ralph, who had also been staring at the floor, looked up with a jerk. "Why what?"

"Why are the game shows fixed?"

"How the hell should I know? Everything's fixed. It's the way the system works."

"They don't look fixed to me."

"What?"

"The game shows."

"What about the game shows?"

24

"'They don't look fixed to me.''

Ralph's lip curled. "What would you know about it?"

Sam looked offended. "I watch them. I watch them all the time. I watch them just the same as you do."

"It's how you watch them. That's what counts."

"You just watch them. There's only one way to watch a game show. You just watch. There ain't no difference between you and me."

"The difference is that you're dumb."

Sam's chubby fingers began to move slowly. It was the first sign of agitation.

"I don't like for you to call me dumb, Ralph."

"That's 'cause you're dumb."

Sam's fingers moved more quickly. He lowered his voice. "I don't like for you to call me dumb, Ralph."

"You want to know why you're dumb, huh? You want to know?"

Sam's baby face was starting to get flushed.

"I'm warning you, Ralph. You didn't ought to talk to me like that. Just 'cause you think you're smart don't give you no right to talk to me like that."

Sam's voice went up in pitch. His breathing got faster. "You're down here, just like me. You ain't got no call to look down on me and call me dumb and shit like that."

Ralph turned away. "Aah, take a pill."

Sam went bright red. "Ralph, I . . .''

Ralph realized he had gone too far. He remembered how big Sam was. He quickly became placating. "Listen, Sam, I was only kidding."

Sam raised his arm as though he was going to strike Ralph. Suddenly he changed his mind and began scratching his head with nervous intensity. There was another long silence. Ralph started hitting his bottle again.

"Are you sure, Ralph?"

Ralph patiently put down his bottle. "Sure about what, Sam?"

"Are you sure you were only kidding about me being dumb?"

Ralph sighed. "Sure I'm sure, Sam."

Again they lapsed into silence. Ralph found himself listening to the high-pitched hum that always filled the vault. Sometimes he thought he could hear voices buried in the sound. He knew he had to watch that kind of thing. Suddenly, Sam butted in on his private thoughts.

"Tell me how the game shows are fixed."

"Huh?"

"Will you tell me how the game shows are fixed, please, Ralph?"

"You really want to know?"

"Sure I do, Ralph. I like to hear you talk."

"Okay then, I'll tell you. Just don't interrupt. I don't want to hear you interrupting with no d—I don't want no questions. Okay?"

"Okay, Ralph."

"This is only a theory, right?"

"Right, Ralph."

"The way I figure it is that the game shows have got to be fixed. I mean, did you ever see an ordinary sort of joe on that kind of show? Huh? Did you ever?"

"I seen a few. Not many, but a few."

"That's where they're clever, see? They put a bum on, now and then, to fool you. Most of the time it's nice, good-looking, young people, young guys and young broads. Everyone's so busy looking at the broads' tits that they don't realize what's being done to them."

Ralph paused to take a drink. He was moving into the drunk and belligerent phase of the day.

"Take the Dreamroad bit. You never see bums like us get as far as the Dreamroad. They're always knocked out in the early rounds. It's only the good lookers who make it onto the Dreamroad."

"Maybe they're the smart ones, Ralph."

"I thought I said for you not to interrupt."

"I'm sorry, Ralph."

"You want to hear this?"

"Yeah, Ralph."

"So don't interrupt."

"I'm sorry, Ralph."

"Okay. Anyway, that's bullshit about them people getting on the Dreamroad because they're smart. That's bullshit, you hear?"

"I hear you, Ralph."

"They get on there because they fuck the producers and directors and casting directors and studio managers and all the other pussy-mouthed fuckers who sit around in NCC and ACC and Trans National. That's why."

Ralph was starting to get worked up.

"You ever noticed how, once they get on the Dreamroad, there's always a good guy and a bad guy? And the bad guy always looks like he's going to win right up until the last minute, and then the good guy wins in the nick of time and all the slobbos at home go to bed pleased. You noticed that, did you?"

"Lots of times it's a broad who wins, Ralph. You said it was always guys."

"I know that, stupid. Good guy's only a figure of speech. Jesus Christ."

"Don't call me stupid, Ralph."

Ralph took a deep breath. "Okay, okay, you're not stupid. But don't that sound like a fix to you? Like they ain't putting on a real show but one that'll keep the dumbbells watching? Huh?"

"I'm not sure, Ralph."

"What ain't you sure about?"

"I don't know, Ralph. All I know is that I'd sure like to win one of those shows." He nodded toward the never-ending rows of cabinets. "I'd sure rather be dreaming like a stiff than sitting here."

"At least sitting here is real. You see what happens.

You really want to be hooked up to a lot of tubes and wires and all, being fed with garbage all day?''

"You wouldn't know about any of that, Ralph. You'd be getting laid and having adventures and all that sort of thing."

"Only inside your head."

"Isn't that where it counts, Ralph?"

Ralph finally lost patience.

"When are you going to get it through your head that you ain't never, ever, going to get inside one of these cabinets?''

Ralph banged his fist on the nearest cabinet. Sam suddenly beamed as though a wonderful idea had just struck him.

"I could always win a game show."

Ralph practically screamed at him. "I've been telling you for the last fucking hour, the game shows are fixed! Got it? Fixed!"

Sam thoughtfully shook his head. "I ain't sure about that, Ralph.''

HELEN MCDONALD HAD BEEN HOOKED to a feelie for so long that her own memories and personality never drifted to the surface. In the private, subjective world of her own mind she was Thongar the Planet Waster, the scourge of the galaxy. Helen McDonald had always wanted to be a man. That was the one thing that her wealthy family and expensive upbringing had been unable to change, until, that is, the feelies had come along.

"First on the block in a box," she had told her friends

gaily as she had left for her lifelong appointment at the feelie office. She had been a hundred percent sure that she would rather spend the rest of her life as Thongar the Planet Waster than as Helen McDonald.

Thongar was no ordinary man. Physically he was a giant. He stood over seven feet tall in his black space armor. His IQ was well into the two hundreds and he commanded the three hundred crew of the starship *Vixen* with a will of iron.

Thongar was one of the last free privateers of the galaxy. Lesser men called him a pirate, but Thongar cared nothing for the opinions of lesser men. Thongar took what he wanted without hesitation or regret. It didn't matter if it was a woman, a treasure, or even an entire planet.

For years, the Federation starfleet had hunted him in vain. Only two days earlier Thongar had outthought, outmaneuvered, and outgunned the captain of the heavy cruiser *Exeter*. The *Exeter* now hung in deep space, a dead, silent hulk of fused metal. The *Vixen* moved, like a black-hulled, monstrous vulture, in a tight orbit on the night side of yet another unsuspecting planet that was marked by Thongar for rape and plunder.

He sat tensely in his command chair on the *Vixen*'s bridge. His strong features betrayed none of his anxiety. Absently he fingered the deep white scar that ran vertically down one side of his face. The sword cut that had made the scar had also cost him his right eye. The empty socket was covered by the black lens of an implanted sensor.

The helmsman turned and looked at Thongar. "Beam down minus ten seconds, Captain."

Thongar hit the communicator stud on the arm of his chair. "Transporter room?"

"Yo!"

"First wave of ground attack ready to beam down?"

"All ready, Skipper."

"Commence."

"Aye, Skipper."

The planet that lay beneath the *Vixen* was a small, arid world. It had been halfheartedly colonized during the years of the great exodus. All that remained of that were some half a million inhabitants. About a third of these lived in the only city that had grown up around the planet's single shuttle port.

The rest of these displaced Earthmen were spread over the surface of the planet. They were ragged prospecting miners looking for instant wealth in the rich but scattered lodes of dilithium crystal that were this world's only resource.

Thongar also intended to find himself a fortune in dilithium. He was simply going about getting it in a much more direct way. If it had been a bigger planet it might have been necessary to subdue it with prolonged phaser fire from out of orbit. As it was, with such a small population, no storm of fire was needed. A sudden surprise attack by ground-level shock troops would be more than enough to seize control.

Thongar stood up. "I'm going to join the second wave down planetside. Take over, Number One."

Juno the Cruel moved toward the control chair. She was a tall, statuesque woman. Her skin had the distinctive blue tinge that was characteristic of those who had grown up in the Vegan settlements. Many years before, she and Thongar had been lovers. Now they were just comrades in arms.

At the door to the ship's elevator, Thongar was met by his servant Y'dug. The tiny figure bent under the weight of the black-winged pressure helmet and the heavy belt that held Thongar's hand phaser and power ax. These made up the rest of Thongar's battle equipment.

As Thongar entered the transporter room, the second wave of shock troops were preparing to beam down. The privateers wore no regular uniforms. That was for the lackeys of the Federation. Although all of the privateers' armor was similar in design, the function dictated this, each had embellished his own in unique individual style. The space armor was painted, engraved, and decorated with baroque figures. It was as though super technology and barbarian splendor had clashed head on.

A huge man in red armor with inlaid, and mainly obscene, figures all over it detached himself from the mass. Two horns curved out from his helmet. It was Hengist the Red. He and Thongar had been together since their earliest days on the privateer space lanes. He clapped a huge mailed hand on Thongar's shoulder.

"Are you coming down with us for the kill, Skipper?"

Thongar looked at the man who even towered over him. He knew that the body inside the red armor was at least half made up of artificial replacements for flesh and bone that had been blown or hacked away in a thousand privateer battles.

Thongar smiled one of his rare smiles. There was no humor in it. "Yes, I'm coming down with you."

Hengist looked around at the other men waiting to board the transporter. "You hear that, lads? The skipper's coming with us."

Thongar's helmet radio was jammed with cheering and laughter as he strode toward the transporter. The machine flickered and glowed with static as the warriors were beamed down in groups of ten.

It was a scene from hell that met Thongar's eyes as he reassembled on the surface of the planet. Punching the servo controls on the hip of his suit, and thumbing off the safety of his power ax, Thongar instantly became a part of it. With the suit's motors boosting his own combat-hardened muscles, he made for the thickest of the fighting with great twenty-foot bounds.

Already the battle was almost over. Buildings were burning and most of the civilian population was running in aimless panic, looking for a place to escape the phaser

beams and swinging blades of the savage invaders. The
only real resistance was coming from a few small groups
of uniformed men. Thongar presumed they were either
local police or militia.

Some way to his left, five of them were attempting to
set up a photon cannon. Thongar swerved in midstride
and raced toward them. He smiled grimly at the men's
agitation as they worked desperately to assemble the
weapon before the deadly figure in black armor and
winged helmet could reach them.

The power ax seemed to take on a life of its own as
Thongar squeezed the grip. It struck the first defender on
the shoulder and, with hardly any effort on the part of
the wielder, almost cut him vertically in two.

A second defender pulled a phaser from his belt.
Thongar manipulated the grip on his ax. The man's arm
was transformed into a bloody stump. On the return
swing a third man lost his head. Seeing the fate of their
companions, the remaining two began to run. Thongar
coolly burned them down with his own phaser, then he
sprang away in search of fresh slaughter.

He rounded the corner of a high-rise building. Flames
gushed from the upper stories, causing a sinister flick-
ering glow to illuminate the fighting. He was poised to
launch himself on another superhuman leap when a girl
burst from the building and ran straight into him. Almost
as a reflex Thongar seized her in one steel-gloved fist.
Two armored privateers came storming out of the building in hot pursuit. They pulled up short when they saw
Thongar holding her. If he had been another privateer,
they might have argued over the girl. Nobody argued with
Thongar.

For the first time, the Planet Waster looked down at
the girl who still fought against his merciless grip. She
had flaming red hair and an attractive, independent face.
Her clothes were sufficiently torn and disheveled to re-

veal that her body was pliantly rounded and very desirable. Thongar laughed one of his humorless laughs.

Dragging the still resisting girl behind him, Thongar started off in a new direction. His objective was a small, almost undamaged, single-story building. He kicked in the door with a power-assisted foot and routinely sprayed the interior with rapid phaser fire.

A fast look around assured him that the place was, in fact, empty. The girl continued to fight him, beating on the breastplate of his armor with her free hand. He kicked the door shut behind him and threw the girl roughly into a corner. She leapt up and tried to run for the door. Thongar laughed and hurled her back again. She made a second attempt to get up, but then seemed to change her mind. She lay back on the floor and turned her face away from the black-clad giant. It was as though she realized that further resistance was useless.

With a grim, satisfied smile, Thongar broke the seals on his space armor.

"IE IS DREAMS MADE FLESH
is fantasy made real
is everything you ever wanted."

Barney Rooter liked the feelie commercials. He wasn't all that keen on the audio. He would rather turn off the TV sound and put on a solid tension tape. He did like the visuals, though, the soft, rounded, abstract shapes that weren't really anything but suggested everything. Even the colors seemed to offer all kinds of not-quite defined delights.

Barney Rooter wished the feelie commercials went on

longer. He would really dig to lie back and just watch them, the latest tension tape pumping out while he snurfed on a can of Solvex until he was totally jammed up. That would be really neat.

One time, when his folks were away, some of his friends had come around. They had tried to get a visual like a feelie commercial by pulling the TV out of its wall mounting and messing around with the insides. They had honked up some of the old Solvex and it had been great, while it lasted. Trying to put the set back to normal at the same time as dealing with a Solvex comedown was beyond them. All they had managed to do was completely unsync the picture. When they had wanted to watch *Wildest Dreams*, all they had gotten were random shapes.

When his folks came home, his dad had really had his hide.

WANDA-JEAN HAD THOUGHT IT WAS GO-ing to be glamorous. In fact, it had felt more like being inducted into the military. She had called the number specified in the letter and been issued with a reference number and an appointment for four days later at nine-thirty in the morning. It was another day off work, and she was very well aware that she was coasting mightily close to being fired. Her supervisor, that old cow Hendrikson, had long ago stopped buying her one-day illnesses. It couldn't be helped, though. A chance to be on "Wildest Dreams" and maybe win a feelie contract for the rest of her life was more than worth the risk. She had been a little surprised that the phone at

NCC had been answered by a computer that was programmed to only recognize her name and relay the next
set of instructions. Its final words had been strictly for
idiots.

"Do not forget or lose your reference number. Without that number, your contestant consideration will be
automatically canceled."

Wanda-Jean's pride had suffered a further deflation
when she had arrived for the first appointment. She had
been shown to a large room on the ground floor of the
NCC tower by a harassed PA whose curt manner verged
on rudeness. To her dismay, she discovered that there
were fifty or more people in the room. The invitation
hadn't been to automatic fortune and fame but to a total
cattle call. How many were they going to pick out of all
those people? Five? Ten? It couldn't be more. She was
tempted to walk away from what looked to be a mainly
hopeless situation, but a certain resolve she had never
suspected she possessed kept her going. She had already
lost a day's work, so what the hell. Someone had to win.

For the next hour she filled out a lengthy question-
naire, which grilled her on a great many personal details
that she felt were hardly anybody's business, let alone
NCC's and the producers of "Wildest Dreams." With an
inborn natural caution, she lied a good deal about her
lifestyle, making herself appear much more the apple-pie
American girl that she never was in reality. The ques-
tionnaire was followed by an equally long general knowledge quiz. As she worked her way through it she
suspected that the questions had been rigged to provide
a further personality profile, but she was hard enough
pressed just coming up with answers to practice any kind
of deceit or duplicity.

For the final stage the applicants were taken, one by
one, into a side room and given a brief video test. After
that they were told that if they were selected for the physical challenge test, they would be contacted by phone.

Then they were directed to the street, and that was it. The anticlimax was crushing. It was lunchtime and Wanda-Jean had nothing to do with the afternoon except to go home and watch the soaps. After five days, she had given up all hope. Either her personal profile didn't fit, or she had screwed up the test, or maybe she just looked plain bad on the video. With her luck, she had probably failed all three. It was only an illogical belief in long-shots that kept her from throwing away the slip of paper on which she had written her reference number. It was thus that it came as something of a major surprise to pick up the phone a full week later and hear a real-live human being announce herself as Garvey Asher, Associate Producer of "Wildest Dreams."

"Wanda-Jean, do you still have your reference number?"

"Yes, I do."

"I'm happy to tell you, Wanda-Jean, that you have been selected from your intake group to go forward to the next level of selection. Are you still interested in becoming a contestant?"

Strangely, Wanda-Jean's first thought was that it would mean missing another goddamn day of work. Hendrikson was hard on her back, and one more day would most likely be her final one. The panic lasted only a moment.

"Yes, of course, I really want to be a contestant more than anything in the world."

Garvey Asher informed her that she should report to the NCC studio complex in three days' time and be prepared to remain for the whole day. She should dress as if for the gym. The call was six in the morning. The studios were all the way out in Nettlewood, and Wanda-Jean realized that to get there so early she would have to take a cab. It would cost her a small fortune, and getting back, particularly if it was late, didn't bear thinking about. The cab, on top of the pink and black Actionskin and the new pair of Converse HiFlyers that she decided she had to go out and purchase for the tryout, was turning this into an expensive hobby.

When she arrived at the studios, bleary-eyed from having dragged herself out of bed at four A.M., just three hours after she had crawled into it, she discovered that once again it was a cattle call—although this time there were only about thirty hopefuls. Every one of them seemed in peak condition. They all looked like tennis pros, aerobic instructors, or dancers, and all were dressed in the very latest and sexiest workout wear. Wanda-Jean's heart sank.

First each would-be contestant was required to sign a lengthy release form by which they absolved the producers of "Wildest Dreams," NCC, and all of its affiliates from any liability resulting from death or injury during the course of the show or while testing for the show. On that cheerful note, they were divided into groups of seven and told to get changed. Wanda-Jean was so outraged that she almost spoke up about it. After all the money she had spent, she wasn't going to get to wear the Actionskin after all! The only consolation was that the other contestants were also being stripped of their chic workout wear. As each one of them entered the changing room, he or she was handed one of the skintight bodysuits that was the uniform of contestants on the actual show itself.

The costume was one more small moment of truth. Like the costumes on the real show these were made from the specially constructed and highly unstable material that dissolved when wet. There was a lot of water involved in "Wildest Dreams," and seminudity was a big part of the show. How she felt about being naked or almost naked on national TV was something that Wanda-Jean had not expected to have to confront so early in the proceedings. She knew that it would be expected of her if she actually got on the show, but she had postponed thinking about it, rather hoping that it would take care of itself. The costume was minimal enough to start with,

a skimpy, skintight, one-piece bathing suit cut high on
the hips. But at this point, there was only one choice:
She simply went with the flow and changed along with
the rest. Then when everyone was ready, they were led
out in their groups of seven to the physical challenge set.

There was something threatening and inhuman about
the "Wildest Dreams" physical challenge course. It was
something she had never noticed all the times she had
watched the show. On the TV screen it looked like fun.
In reality, it was just plain threatening. The long, straight
avenue, flanked by the high tiers of spectator seats,
seemed deliberately planned to reduce the players who
would race down it to the level of experimental animals
in a vast sterile lab.

The tests were being conducted on an old set, one from
three seasons before. Only a minimal number of the
lighting effects were up, but even without the assault of
garish color, the set looked formidable. Overhead, silent
figures watched from the electricians' catwalks in the roof
of the sound stage. Wanda-Jean suppressed a shudder.
She wondered if the other contestants felt the same. They
were all avoiding each other's eyes. Loudspeakers called
them in turn.

"Will all contestants in group four move up to the
starting gate?"

That was her. Wanda-Jean moved along with the other
six in her group in the direction of the shining aluminum
starting gates. She looked fixedly ahead toward the far
end of the course.

"Will contestants all make sure that they go directly
to the gate that corresponds with the number on your
costume."

There was a number five between Wanda-Jean's
breasts. She headed for gate five.

"This is the elimination part of the process. Of the
seven of you, only two will be eligible to go on to the

broadcast show. Good luck. Now move right up to the gates, please.''

Wanda-Jean stepped into the small space that was her part of the starting gate. The row of horizontal metal bars in front of her reflected the multicolored studio lights. She could see tiny distorted images of herself in their polished surface. Again she had the feeling of being an animal. This time, she was in a cage, an exhibit in some incredibly expensive zoo.

''Twenty seconds to the Question.''

At that moment, twenty seconds seemed like a lifetime. The floor manager who was calling the orders swung high overhead, perched on a mobile crane. Two more cranes carried the elevated cameras. More cameras were deployed on both sides and at the end of the course. Wanda-Jean felt the lenses staring at her like the collective, unwinking eyes of a hundred million people.

''Once the Question has been given, you have ten seconds to consider the alternative answers.''

Wanda-Jean stared down the course. It seemed impossibly long. It never looked that long on television. For a moment she panicked. She'd never even make it to the end, let alone onto the correct answer spot. The chrome nozzles of the high-pressure hoses stared back at her.

''Once the gates are sprung you have twenty seconds to reach the correct answer spot. The hoses will come on when the leading contestant crosses the halfway line.''

The first part of the course was easy. All you had to do was run like hell. When the hoses came on, then it got rough. You had to keep going straight into them. The hoses tracked from side to side in a random pattern. If you were clever, you could dodge the worst of the barrage of water. If you didn't, you'd be knocked off your feet.

''Ten seconds to the Question.''

Wanda-Jean made an effort to get herself under control.

"Five seconds."

The bleachers on either side of the course were empty. If it had been a real show, they'd have been filled with screaming game fans. On auditions, they simply ran a recorded crowd track to simulate the audience.

Wanda-Jean knew this game was Dreamroad standard. She had seen it featured in the show more than once. She also knew it was a tough one. She smoothed down her suit. She might as well look good to start with. Once the water hit her, the synthetic material would start to dissolve.

"And now, boys and girls, here comes the Question!"

The voice had changed. It was the familiar cry of Bobby Priest, Mr. Wildest Dreams. Like the crowd track, on auditions he too was recorded.

"What is the current population of the planet Earth? Is it A—three billion, B—eight billion, or C—five billion? You now have ten seconds to consider the Question."

Wanda-Jean had another moment of panic. Which was the correct answer? Then it came to her. It was C. She was sure she had seen it on TV quite recently. She looked down to the far end of the course, at the three circular, illuminated podia on which the players had to stand to signify their answers. She had to make it to the right one within the twenty seconds to have even a chance of getting on the show.

"Five seconds."

The tension was unbearable. Wanda-Jean felt herself start to tremble. The only consolation was that in less than a minute she would know, one way or the other.

An alarm went off and lights flashed. The gate in front of Wanda-Jean snapped open with a metallic clang. The crowd recording came on. It was deafeningly loud, almost at the threshold of pain. Wanda-Jean tried to shut it out as she sprang from the starting gate. She was running as though her life depended on it. The other contestants were all around her. A well-built girl beside her ran straight across her path. Wanda-Jean was forced to slow down, otherwise the two of them would have gone down in a tangle of arms and legs.

There were four players in front of Wanda-Jean. That meant she was third from last. She'd never make it through to the actual show if she couldn't pull up. She forced her legs to pump still harder. The blood pounded in her head. It was accompanied by the almost unbearable crowd noise. Watching "Wildest Dreams" on TV, she'd never noticed how many of the crowd yelled really disgusting obscenities.

The muscular young man who was leading the field crossed the halfway line. The water came on. Almost immediately a jet hit him squarely in the midriff. He folded up, staggered, and fell. As he tried to get up, another jet sent him sprawling back down the course. His costume was already dissolving into rags.

Wanda-Jean had no time to worry about other people's troubles. She was now within range of the high-pressure nozzles. Two of them were sweeping her part of the course like crossfire. The girl in front of her jumped to avoid one of the two waterjets and slammed into Wanda-Jean.

"Cunt!"

The word came out like a gasp of quickly expelled breath. The girl jammed her elbow into Wanda-Jean's ribs and tried to trip her into the path of the other jet.

"Bitch."

Wanda-Jean swore almost as a reflex and twisted her fingers in the girl's bleached hair. More by luck than judgment, she pulled the girl off balance. She tottered backward for a couple of steps, straight into the full force of the jets. Wanda-Jean went on running, smiling as the other girl was spun, flat on her back with windmilling arms and legs, the wrong way down the now slippery course.

Wanda-Jean's jubilation was short-lived, however. A third jet swung toward her. She did her best to sidestep, but she wasn't quite fast enough. She didn't take the full force of it, but even the periphery of the stream was enough to spin her around and hurl her against the track. The impact of the water was like simultaneously being punched by a giant fist and stabbed by a thousand freezing needles. Most of the front of her suit had simply vanished at the first touch of wetness.

It was all too much. Wanda-Jean was defeated. Cold, wet, and half-naked, she saw no point in going on. She had blown her chance. The recorded voices of the non-existent crowd beat on her head. She wanted to crouch by the wall and cry. Then suddenly everything changed.

There was a clear path all the way to the podia. All the jets seemed to be moving in directions that would not get her. Screwing up her very last reserves, Wanda-Jean sprinted for the finish.

Her surprise at finishing the course almost stopped her. For a split second her mind went blank. She couldn't remember the answer. Then it came to her. C, that was the one. She swerved and jumped onto the C podium.

The muscular young man plunged out of the spray of water. He climbed onto the podium marked B. As he straightened up, completely naked, a siren went off and a hundred lights flashed. The twenty seconds were up. It had seemed like a lifetime to Wanda-Jean.

A hush fell over the recorded crowd as attendants helped the five contestants who hadn't made it off the course. There was just Wanda-Jean and the young man. The voice of Bobby Priest came back again.

"Okay, kids, just so you know you're getting a fair shake on "Wildest Dreams," you've got three seconds, I'll repeat that, three seconds to change your minds."

The crowd noise rose again. The amplified voices were baying either to move or to stay put. Wanda-Jean glanced at the young man. She decided that he was kind of cute.

Neither of them moved. The crowd was cut off as the three-second siren sounded.

Bobby Priest's voice boomed out again.

"And now, what we've all been waiting for!"

A small, clear voice piped up inside Wanda-Jean's head. It said: Emote. You still won't make it if you don't look right.

"The answer to the Question!"

Wanda-Jean dutifully twisted her hands and looked as though she was suffering the worst agonies of suspense.

"The current population of the world is . . . wait for it . . . yes! Answer C! Five billion!"

Wanda-Jean emoted as fully as she could. She put all her remaining strength into leaping for joy as the lights went up around her. Afterward she was never clear whether she had been putting it on or doing it for real.

"ARE YOU COMING TO BED?"

Mallory was already wearing the black semi-transparent negligee from Beneath It All. Dustin was still dressed, hunched in the conversation pit with his arms wrapped around his knees. The only things he had discarded were the coat and tie that he had worn to dinner. He knew what she wanted, but, perversely, he didn't feel like playing the game. Dinner with the Fedders had been a tedious exercise in pretentious snobbery, and he wanted a little time to himself. Martin Fedder was a shallow little social climber, and wife Laramie was just plain stupid. Dustin was worn out from doing what was expected of him. He had tried to weasel out of the Fedders' invitation, but Mallory had insisted. For some reason she believed that Laramie Fedder might be of help to her in landing the Krebs account. Dustin couldn't see it himself. About the only thing that Laramie Fedder had ever landed was the unspeakable Martin, and she was welcome to him. Now that the evening chez Fedder had been endured, Mallory expected Dustin to retire to the bedroom and give her a half hour of his undivided and energetic attention.

He shook his head. "I think I'm going to sit and watch TV for a while."

Dustin was aware that TV was becoming his equivalent of a headache. Mallory was silhouetted against the light from the bathroom door. She looked good, but his mood wouldn't let him respond. When she spoke, there was an edge to her voice that indicated that if he kept this up, he would pay dearly sometime in the near future.

"TV? Do you feel okay?"

"I think I drank a little too much of Martin's port."

"Being a little drunk never slowed you down before."

"I feel more queasy than drunk. Besides, I want to watch Bones Bolt."

"Bones Bolt? Are you kidding? You're going to turn yourself into an imbecile. That show is nothing but hysterical garbage."

"We have to stay aware of garbage."

"That's bullshit, Dustin, and you know it."

Dustin was aware of her slim legs, narrow waist, and full breasts. If Mallory hadn't been such a deadly combination of self-interest and ambition, she would have been perfect. He wanted her right then and there, but he wanted much more to prove a point.

"He's doing a piece on the feelies. Renfield of Combined Media is going to be on it."

Mallory practically spat. "The feelies! I'm so sick of that word."

She stalked off to the bedroom, slamming the door behind her. He would definitely pay in the morning, if not later that night. He sighed and reached for the remote.

The theme had already started. The crushing electronic pulse of the pressure drop instrumental was cranked up to pain threshold. The crowd in the pit were baying right along with it, and at regular intervals they would break into the unique ululation that was the hallmark of Bones Bolt's audience in the pit—what Dustin always referred to as the monkey noise. The cameras panned slowly across the faces of the crowd members who were already in the first throes of controlled hysteria. They were mainly male and mainly in their teens and early twenties. Later in the show, they were likely to become violently physical, a behavior that was tacitly encouraged. The set for "The Bones Bolt Show" was deliberately grim. One critic had likened it to a "stark prison from outer space that happens to be in the middle of a major inmate uprising." The focal point of the set was the pit itself, the circular central area that contained the noisy and frequently angry audience. They were quite literally walled in. Dustin was of the opinion that this was probably the best place for them. Young, unchecked, inner-city males were the greatest fear of a middle class that felt itself increasingly under siege. The audience was surrounded by a circular wall, some eight feet high, designed to resemble massive riveted steel, like the hull plates of a battleship. The flat top of the wall provided a podium for Bolt and his invited guests. Blinding white spotlights constantly circled as though searching for signs of trouble, adding to the all-over jailbreak ambience and creating a sense of frenetic confusion. A narrow catwalk extended out from the wall like a bridge, over the heads of the crowd. It was from there that Bolt communed with his people and, when the spirit moved him, urged them to greater excesses.

The theme faded and Bones Bolt made his grand entrance. His face leaned into the camera in massive close-up.

"Okay! Shut up!"

Bones Bolt was a larger-than-life figure. He was wearing what appeared to be a kind of dark green satin cowl that, coupled with the heavy gold chains that always hung around his neck no matter what the costume, gave him the appearance of a bizarre African monk or maybe a black Ku Klux Klansman with his hood thrown back, which was a very weird concept in itself. Instead of shutting up, the mob in the pit only bayed louder. Bolt advanced along the catwalk over the heads of the faithful. He leaned over the guardrail, his attitude threatening.

"I said *shut up! Shut the fuck up!*"

Bones Bolt had almost single-handedly forced the FCC to forget about their seven deadly words doctrine. Much of his style went all the way back to the old rolling bucket school of rowdy twentieth-century TV preachers like Swaggart, Sharpton, or the Rev. Ike, but his delivery was all his own.

"If you rowdy motherfuckers don't *shut the fuck up* . . . you won't be hearing what we *got* on the *show* for you *tonight*!"

The audience noise subsided. Dustin suspected that the quieting of the mob had a great deal more to do with a good audio mixer than the force of Bones's personality, even though Bones was hardly lacking in that department.

"Tonight we are going to look at the feelies."

There was a roar from the crowd.

"That's right, brothers and sisters, *the feelies*!"

He straightened up, fist clenched to the sky.

"You *hear* me up there in the towers? You *hear* me, Combined Media? You *hear* me, CM? Tonight, you going to hear Bones Bolt and *tremble*!"

Another roar. The visual cut to a close-up of Madison Renfield—the caption read: "Senior Vice President of

Combined Media.'' Renfield, the archetype of the self-satisfied and somewhat faceless corporate spokesman, looked as though he was wishing profoundly that he were anywhere but just a few feet from that sea of young, sweating, angry faces. There was a common question as to which was the more certain suicide: going on ''The Bones Bolt Show,'' or refusing the invitation.

Bones, in the center of the catwalk, was still invoking the gods of video. ''Tonight we're going to find out for you *exactly* what is going on inside those *fancy* downtown buildings where the *rich folks* dream away their lives while homeboys like us can only *walk by and wonder*.''

Bones probably had enough money to spend the next three centuries in a feelie, but he still pretended on the air that he was the ass-out-of-his-pants, inner-city home boy. Bones Bolt was possibly one of the most unlikely individuals ever to get on television. He had first come to the public's attention during the Vaccaville Correction Complex crisis. He had been serving fifteen to life for armed robbery, and as the twenty-nine-day standoff ground on between armed convicts on one side and riot police, FBI, federal troops, and National Guard on the other, Bones had quickly become the outspoken and flamboyant leader of the more moderate faction in the prisoners' negotiating committee. As such, he had started appearing on TV on a nightly basis. Once the emergency was over, following the bloody storming of what was, at the time, the most modern, state-of-the-art penal facility in the whole of the country, Bones Bolt came out a hero. The media credited him with personally being responsible for saving the lives of at least twenty of the hostage guards and civilian administrators. Although a good deal of doubt was later cast on Bones's role, it wasn't before he had received a presidential pardon. It was Taras Karamazov, at the time the wunderkind program director at TBN, who had come up with the idea of giving Bones his own talk show. Despite a storm of protest, ''The Bones

Bolt Show,'' and its explosive combination of populism, radicalism, and racism, seemed to strike a nerve cluster in the collective consciousness. People couldn't resist watching him. He set and broke ratings records and developed an almost fanatical following that was quite prepared to put sponsors out of business if they so much as hinted that they might be thinking of dropping Bones. Himmler Beer learned that to its cost when its largest Denver warehouse went up in flames after Joseph Himmler himself had withdrawn their advertising in a snit following a Bones show on the cult of multiracial pornography. The rest was so much a part of media history that individuals like Madison Renfield now felt it necessary to risk health and sanity to come on the show and justify their position for an audience of sociopaths.

Bones had turned and was coming back to Renfield. He was looking at the company man as though examining a specimen for the first time and not really liking what he was seeing.

''Now this smooth person here, brothers and sisters, he goes by the name of Madison Renfield and is something called a senior vice president at CM, and he's come along here tonight I guess to try and convince us that all those white boys over at CM are real nice guys only working for the best public interest.''

There were shouts from the crowd in the pit.

''We ain't convinced!''

''We ain't *convinced*, motherfucker!''

Dustin, like most other media watchers, had heard how Bones's audience was heavily seeded with paid performers who would start those responses on hidden cue.

Renfield was attempting to look calm and collected but only managed to come off as frightened. Bones was standing beside him, introducing him—or maybe demonstrating the specimen—to the crowd.

''Now, as we all know, CM is the corporation that has the monopoly on the production and distribution of the feelies, and as a result of this monopoly, they can charge exactly what they want for the service. Maybe the first thing we ought to ask Brother Renfield is how come the feelies are so expensive that they're out of the reach of eighty percent of the population.''

In the conversation pit, Dustin hugged his knees and wondered about a feelie. In public, he and Mallory always scoffed at the idea of a feelie—"technology and bad taste conspiring to take escapism to a pathological level''—but secretly he wasn't so sure. There was something very appealing about the prospect of sinking into a tailormade dream and never waking up.

Renfield's eyes flicked from side to side as he cleared his throat and tried to be heard above the noise of the mob. "First of all, Bones, let's get one thing straight. The feelies, or as we prefer to call them, integrated entertainment media, IE for short, are actually not really all that expensive.''

Bones Bolt glared at the company man. "Sure seem expensive to me.''

"Well, they aren't cheap, but when you take into account the cost of plant and production and the expense of maintaining a human being in permanent or semipermanent sleep state, they also aren't that particularly expensive.''

There was a sudden close-up of a sweating Hispanic face. "Sure look expensive from where I'm standing, Jack!''

There were shouts from nearby.

"Right!''

"Yeah, right.''

"Dammit.''

Renfield attempted to go on. "As far as the monopoly is concerned, that was by no means our idea. When the IE system was out of the testing stage we had to apply to the FCC for a special license to market the service. At that time, it was agreed that only one corporation should control the process until a full socioenvironmental study could be concluded."

This time the close-up heckler was a white kid with limp blond hair and long sideburns. "So you bought the government. What else is new?"

The kid was replaced by a Bones looking less than convinced. "That was *five* years ago, man. You telling me that they *still* doing this motherfucking study?"

"It will be some time until we can really assess the long-term effects."

"And what do you guys up at CM expect those results to be, if and when this mighty study finally gets completed?"

"I'm quite confident that they'll show that IE is responsible for a whole spectrum of social benefits on all levels."

Renfield permitted himself a small half smile. He was clearly very pleased with his answer. That was a mistake. It only made the crowd madder than they were already. The pit was bellowing and shaking its fists. Bones swung away from Renfield as though in disgust and pointed dramatically around the curve of the wall.

"Is that a *fact*, Brother Renfield? You are *confident*? Well, along here we have someone who may not be quite as *confident* as you are."

Mark Sturm was leaning nonchalantly on the guardrail. Mark Sturm was a regular guest on "The Bones Bolt Show." As far as Dustin was concerned, the man was nothing but a troublemaker. Sturm had started his career as a stand-up comic with a taste for abusing corporations, but after his mouthing off had become increasingly pointed, he had found that disgruntled executives were starting to drop him pieces of dirt to include in his act. From a mere comic, he was transformed into a man in the know, a man who could at least give an inspired guess as to where the bodies were buried. He was courted by news and talk shows. He developed a research staff and became a definite thorn in the side of the corporations. Many of his researchers were attractive young women— all volunteers—understandable, as Sturm was tall and handsome, a somewhat beak-nosed Errol Flynn with shoulder-length brown hair, every inch the debonair swashbuckler.

Mark Sturm nodded and smiled to Bones. "Hey, Bones, how you doing?"

The two of them slapped hands. The crowd's cheering for Sturm was only slightly less deafening than it had been for Bones himself. Sturm was nothing if not in solid for the underdog and underclass. Bones greeted him like a brother. "I was doing fine, Mark, until I started finding out about this *feelie bullshit*." He indicated Renfield. "This *individual right here* wants me to *believe* that if ever this government report on the feelies comes in, it's going to be *roses*. You *agree* with that?"

Sturm hesitated slightly before he answered. He looked almost sad, as though constantly perplexed by the depths of corporate perfidy.

"Well, Bones, the truth is that there never will be any report. It's like our friend in the pit said. They bought the government."

A medium shot of the pit going ape was followed by a close-up of Renfield starting to inflate.

"That's slander."

Sturm treated Renfield to a look of total contempt. "So sue me. You know damn well that nobody in CM gives a two-cent damn about the long-term effects of the feelies. What do you call the people that you've sold feelies to? Stiffs. Am I right? That's how you refer to your valued clients, isn't it?" He turned to the mob. Sturm was a master at reducing even complex problems down to bite-sized dramatic pieces. "There are two categories. Tempstiffs, the short-term contracts, and permastiffs, the ones who've gone in for life. Stiffs. Think about it."

He addressed the camera directly. "How can anything

be of social benefit when it takes perfectly good minds and reduces them to dreaming zombies? That's worse than any kind of dope you can get on the street. All I can say is thank God it's the rich folks that are getting fucked up for a change.''

The pit was howling. A kid tried to scale the wall to get to Renfield, but Bones's security moved in and pushed him back. Bones's security was made up of big steroid types. They wore white T-shirts and black pants. The words DON'T FUCK WITH MR. ZERO were printed across their T-shirts. There was a new weird slogan for each show. Kids in the street copied them onto their own shirts.

Sturm pointed an accusing finger. "All these bastards at CM want to know about is their goddamn profits." He looked to the mob and produced a sheaf of papers. "You want me to read a bit from their annual report?"

Renfield struggled to be heard. "Since when was it a crime in this country to make a profit? We have worked in full cooperation with the unions to insure—"

He was howled down.

At that point, Mallory came out of the bedroom. "What the hell do you think you're doing?"

Dustin looked up, almost guiltily. "Just watching TV."

"My God, Dustin, you're watching Bones Bolt and Mark Sturm. The next thing, you'll be watching 'Wildest Dreams.' Have you gone crazy? Do you realize how this makes me *feel*?"

Dustin sighed and thumbed the power off. If he didn't go to bed, he would never hear the last of it. As he stood up, he wondered what it would be like to just sink into a feelie and not have to deal with the rest of the world.

◈ "YOU REALIZE THAT WE AIN'T SEEN Artie in something like three days?"

Sam squinted into the far distance of the vault, as though he expected Artie suddenly to appear because he'd noticed his absence. Ralph shrugged and picked up his broom.

"His goofing off will get him fired, one of these days."

"The union won't let him get fired, will they, Ralph?" Sam looked mildly concerned for Artie.

Ralph leaned on his broom. "The union won't do nothing for him if they find out he's missing off the job more times than he shows up. He'll be out on his ass, and nobody'll say a word."

Sam scratched his armpit with a perplexed air. "That'd be too bad."

Ralph blinked. "Huh?"

"It'd be a shame if they fired Artie."

"Why?"

"What do you mean, why?" Sam appeared to be shocked. "I mean, he's our partner. We work with him. I'd miss him if he got fired."

"But we never see him. How the hell can you miss a guy you don't ever see, for Christ's sake?"

"I'd miss not knowing if he was around somewhere. I guess you could say I'd miss not seeing him."

"You know something, Sam?"

"What, Ralph?"

"You ain't fucking normal, Sam. You ain't normal at all." Ralph pushed his broom idly under one of the feelie cabinets.

53

Sam stood staring at him. "Wouldn't you miss Artie if he got fired?"

"Like hell I would. He's a fucking psycho and he gives me the creeps, prowling around here, out of sight. God knows what he does out there."

"You think he does all those things he tells us about? You think he's really interfering with the women?!!"

Ralph shrugged. "I don't know if he's raping the stiffs or not. I've never seen any signs of it."

"You never move more than a couple of rows from here. He could be doing all kinds of weird shit in other parts of the vault."

Ralph smiled. "You have just had a very profound thought, Sam."

Sam looked pleased and embarrassed. "I did, Ralph?"

"You forgot something, though."

Sam's face sagged. "I did?"

"If he was messing with the stiffs, they'd monitor something upstairs. He'd have to be pretty smart to unseal the cabinet, open the body bag, and fuck the stiff without unhooking some of the tubes or wires. He'd even have to put the body bag back on and seal the cabinet again. He'd have to be pretty smart."

"Artie's quite smart."

"He couldn't go on fucking stiff after stiff without messing something up."

"Even if he did, they might not notice."

"Sure they'd notice. You know they monitor every stiff."

"They didn't notice that stiff that died on us."

Ralph looked quite shocked. "How come you're so fucking smart today?"

"I don't know. Think I ought to take something?"

Ralph was at a loss for words. He wasn't sure he liked this particular version of Sam. Before he could think about it, the phone on the wall rang. At least Sam didn't move toward the phone. Talking to the upstairs was traditionally Ralph's job. Ralph picked it up.

"5066."

"Bringing down a new client."

"Right now?"

The voice took on a sarcastic edge. "You busy or something?"

Ralph scowled into the phone. "Anytime you like."

"They're on their way."

The connection clicked off, and Ralph hung up. He looked at Sam, who seemed to have come out in a puzzled expression.

"New stiff."

"What?"

"They're bringing down a new stiff from the upstairs."

"A lifer?"

"What else would it be in this section?"

Sam looked around and scratched his head. "I don't see where they're going to put it."

"They'll put it in the cabinet they just took the dead one out of."

"But they didn't do anything to the cabinet. It could be faulty."

"So who gives a fuck?"

"But if the last one died, so could this one."

"You're really being profound today."

Sam looked scared. "I gotta take a Serenax."

He fumbled in his overalls. Ralph leaned on his broom and stared into space. Sam gulped down his pill. Ralph began to hurt for a drink, but he couldn't risk it right now. If the installation crew showed up and caught him with a bottle, it would be him out on his ass instead of Artie. He wasn't quite at the point where he didn't care.

When Sam finally broke the silence his voice was slurred. "I wonder what it'll be like."

Ralph was too busy wondering when Sam would finally take an overdose to hear the remark. "Huh?"

"I said I wonder what it'll be like."

"What what will be like?"

"What the new stiff will be like."

"You interested?"

Sam hesitated. "Yeah . . . sure I am."

"Why?"

"I don't know."

"Oh, come on. You've got to know. What's so fucking interesting about a stiff? Huh?"

Sam twisted about uncomfortably. "I . . ."

"Yeah?"

"I suppose I like to think about what they've given up."

Ralph's face curled into a bullying sneer. "You sure you ain't getting the same itch as your good buddy Artie?"

Sam became indignant. "I ain't sure I like that, Ralph."

Ralph let loose all his needing-a-drink spite on Sam. "Want to get in and fool around with them cold ladies, do you, Sam?"

Sam went bright red. "You got a foul mouth, Ralph."

Ralph's next assault was cut short by the arrival of a golf cart with two clean-cut young men. Ralph noted that although they weren't the two that had taken away the dead stiff, they might just as well have come out of the same mold. The new stiff was on a stretcher on the back of the cart.

"It's another one for your tender loving care."

Ralph scowled. "We'll treat him just like a brother."

"It's not a him, it's a her."

Sam, who had been staring at his fingers, looked up sharply. "A her?"

Ralph gave him a quick sideways leer. "Maybe you are getting like Artie."

Sam went red and opened his mouth to say something. Then he thought better of it and closed it again.

One of the clean-cut young men looked quizzically at them. "What's up with you two?"

Ralph put on a bland smile. "Nothing, just a private joke."

"You vault jockeys get damned odd down here."

"Vault jockeys? Is that what you're calling us upstairs? Who thought up that one?"

The clean-cut man ignored the question. "Where's the cabinet where the stiff died?"

"Back down the row a piece."

Sam looked shocked. "You're not going to put her in there, are you?"

The young man looked at him in blank amazement. "What the hell do you think we're going to do? It's the only empty cabinet in the whole damned vault."

Sam still seemed dully horrified. "It just don't seem right."

The young men weren't interested. They were already reversing the golf cart along the row of cabinets until it was level with the empty one. They jumped out with efficient briskness, disconnected the old control pac, and put in a new one. Next they carefully removed the inert body from the golf cart and placed it in the cabinet. Then they started the complex process of inserting the electrodes and feeder tubes.

Sam and Ralph moved closer. Even Ralph was surprised at the youth of the woman. From what he could see of her face, she was little more than a girl. It was an attractive, doll-like face, with white blond hair like spun sugar. Sam had started to look profoundly unhappy.

When the smart young men had finally finished, they banged down the lid of the cabinet with an air of finality and closed the seal. As they climbed back into the golf cart, the one who had done all the talking couldn't resist a parting shot.

"Try not to let this one die on you, okay?"

Ralph gave them the finger as they drove away. Sam still looked unhappy. Ralph turned on him.

"What the fuck's the matter with you?"

"I was just thinking about that girl."

"You crazy or something?"

"I was just thinking what a girl like that was doing spending the rest of her life in a feelie."

Ralph made an impatient gesture. "Everyone wants to spend their life in a feelie, or hadn't you heard?"

"But she was so young and nice-looking."

"And rich, so what?"

"She must have had so much going for her. What's she want to end up here for?"

"Listen, dummy, she's probably in there being Attila the Hun. No matter what people got, they always think they can get better. That's why feelies got made."

Sam still wasn't happy. "I sure hope Artie doesn't get at her."

DETECTIVE IZZY STEIGER WALKED INTO the squad room of the Ninth Precinct and looked around wearily. Murty and Rojas were sitting behind their desks doing nothing in particular. He dropped into his own empty chair.

"You heard the latest?"

Rojas shook his head. "What's the latest?"

"The Seventh busted a bootleg feelie parlor over on Jay Street."

"What the hell is a bootleg feelie parlor?"

Murphy looked up from doing the *Post* crossword. "I

heard of one of those a couple of years back. They started up again?''

Rojas was still looking baffled. ''How the hell can some sleazo on Jay Street bootleg a feelie? They definitely don't have the technology.''

Steiger picked up a sheaf of arrest reports and then put them back down. The station's climate control was once again out, and it was too hot to work. Out on the street, the temperature must have been over a hundred degrees, with seventy percent humidity. *And the president goes on TV to tell everyone that the greenhouse effect is nothing to worry about,* he thought. *Yeah, right.*

''They don't have the technology, but they have some awful stupid customers.''

Murphy folded up the *Post* and placed it on the desk. ''It's what you could call voodoo technology.''

Rojas got up from his chair and walked over to the water cooler. ''So how do they work this?''

Steiger put his feet up on the desk. ''Basically it's a con. The guys running the scam get hold of a space—a garage, a storefront, whatever, God knows spaces aren't hard to find down around Jay. They build some fake feelie coffins out of lengths of thirty-inch plastic pipe or something of the sort and hook them up to dummy control pacs. Like I said, their customers are pretty stupid, so just about anything will do, the inside of an old TV and a couple of flashing lights, just so long as it looks marginally ''Star Trek.'' Once that's all in place, they start hustling for business.''

Rojas crushed the paper cup he had been drinking from and tossed it backhand into the wastebasket.

''So how do they actually do the feelie? What's the illusion?''

Steiger laughed. ''In a word, crude. The come on is usually sexual, and most of the marks are men. Once they've got the mark in the coffin, they shoot him full of some crap IV cocktail. Usually it's one thing to put them half out and something else that'll make them hallucinate like crazy. Dust and barbiturate, acid and MPTP, Serenax and PCP, synthetic heroin and DMA—I guess pretty much what they can get their hands on.''

Murty grunted. ''You can get your hands on practically anything down there.''

Rojas sat down again. ''Sounds like a class act.''

Steiger went on. ''So once they've got the mark doped out of his mind, they stick a google TV on the front of his face. You know, a Sony Maskman or one of those. They run a porno loop, and at the same time some old whore, one who's probably too fucked up to work the street anymore, gives the guy a blow job.''

Rojas was shaking his head in disbelief. ''Oh, choice. How the hell does anyone fall for this shit?''

Steiger spread his hands in a don't-ask-me gesture. ''What can I tell you? Seems there're fools out there who want to be in a feelie so bad, they'll convince themselves of anything. The experience, if you can call it that, maybe only lasts a few minutes, and they spend the next two or three hours sleeping off the drugs. When it's all over, they wake up with a motherfucker of a headache and no memory but determined to believe that they had a hell of a time.''

''What do they pay for all this?''

''Upward of five hundred.''

Rojas eyebrows shot up. ''Jesus Christ, five hundred bucks for a blow job and a chance to OD.''

Steiger grimaced. ''And the chance to get any one of a half-dozen retroviruses. The way I heard it, the IVs weren't any too sanitary. Like I say, there's fools out there who'll believe anything. Also you'll be able to hear all about it on the late news. Pictures at eleven.''

''Kowalski again?''

''Seems like it. Kowalski of the Seventh, the reporters' friend. I hear he has a smartcard with all the numbers of his press contacts on it. When he wants to tip them off, he doesn't even have to dial.''

Murty's lip curled. ''Good old Kowalski. I don't know why they don't just make him the official PR of the Seventh Precinct.''

Steiger shrugged. ''He's better off as he is. If he went official, he wouldn't make as much money.''

Rojas was furious. ''Kowalski burns my ass. What's with him? He got to spend more time on the phone tipping off the media than doing his fucking job, whatever that might be. Don't he got no dignity?''

Murty spat on the floor. ''He's got to supplement his income somehow.''

Steiger leaned back in his chair. ''You ain't heard it all yet. Kowalski really outdid himself on this one. He didn't only tip the media that this feelie bust was going to go down. He even called out the publicity office of CM. They had cameras down there. They're apparently going to make a commercial out of it, warning the public that the only good feelie is a CM feelie. Kowalski's going to be hired on as a technical advisor.''

Murty laughed. ''So Kowalski's in with CM. He ain't going to be long for the department now. He's going to be moving on to better things.''

Rojas lit a cigarette. ''You guys ever think that what those bootleggers are doing isn't all that different to what CM is doing? I mean, CM is a lot more hygienic, but it's really all the same ball game.''

Murty looked at him sadly. ''You really don't have a clue.''

''What do you mean, I don't have a clue?''

''The world runs on diplomacy, Rojas. It's something you don't appreciate. That's why you're still D2 after seven years, and Kowalski drives a Jaguar.''

Rojas turned away. ''Fuck Kowalski.''

Steiger had walked over and picked up Murty's copy of the *Post*. He idly leafed through it, finally stopping at the ratings for the day. "Today's top feelie is a cop fantasy. You become a police homicide detective."

Murty's eyes rolled heavenward. "It's a wonderful world."

⬠ THUNDER CRASHED AROUND THE apartment building, and through the window, Wanda-Jean could see the lightning repeatedly striking the CM Tower over on the west side. The heat and humidity had temporarily exploded into a violent storm, but nobody who knew the city's weather patterns believed that it would be anything but the most brief relief. As soon as the storm was gone, the streets would be steaming again. Wanda-Jean sat and stared out the window at the bursts of electricity and the gray sheets of rain. She thought about turning on the TV. It was almost time for "Torture Garden." Somehow, though, she couldn't. She had a strange feeling of unease. It had started with the "Wildest Dreams" audition and had been with her ever since. She had been asking herself the same question for the past two days, ever since she had heard that she had made it onto the show. What was she really getting into?

The phone rang. Wanda-Jean looked at it suspiciously. She wasn't expecting anyone to call, particularly not in the middle of a raging storm. She picked it up with a feeling of misgiving.

"Hello?"

"This is building security." The building's security system had one of those annoyingly smooth female cabin-attendant voices.

"What is it?"

"You have a visitor."

Wanda-Jean reached for the remote for the living-room wall TV. "Put him on the screen please."

"If you turn on your TV and switch to channel ninety-seven, I will give you the visual image."

That was another annoying thing about the building's security system. Although it was nowhere near sophisticated enough to actually conduct a conversation, it left pauses between statements, in which a person could sound like an idiot by asking the thing fatuous questions.

The wallscreen came to life, and Wanda-Jean tapped up channel ninety-seven. A man was standing in the lobby. He wore one of those transparent, one-piece, plastic slicks over a dark suit. Water dripped from the slick. She didn't recognize him and spoke into the phone.

"I don't know you, do I?"

There was distorted audio from the lobby in her ear.

"Hello? Wanda-Jean?"

She experienced a moment of panic. Maybe it was some forgotten guy she had met in one of the boom-boom rooms when she had been drunk. "I don't think I know who you are. What do you want?"

"I'm Murray Dorfman, Wanda-Jean."

"I'm sorry, I don't think I know you."

"I'm personal assistant to Mr. Priest. We met at the audition the day before yesterday."

Wanda-Jean's heart jumped into her mouth. Bobby Priest's assistant. What was he doing there?

"Oh, my God, Murray, I'm so sorry. The visual image isn't too good on our system here."

Wanda-Jean was lying. There had been so many young men in dark suits at the audition that they had all become a blur.

"May I come up and speak with you for a couple of minutes?"

Wanda-Jean was instantly anxious to please. "Yes, of course. Take the express elevator to twenty-five."

Wanda-Jean hung up. As she did that, she was struck forcibly by a thought. It took about three minutes plus to ride up to the twenty-fifth floor. He would be there in three minutes and both she and the apartment were in a terminal mess. She dragged a brush quickly through her hair and changed out of her jeans and sweatshirt into a slinky kimono. Then she ran around the apartment picking up the things that were most obviously out of place and adjusting the light. She was about finished when the door buzzed again.

She didn't remember Murray Dorfman at all. It was quite conceivable that he might have been at the audition, but he certainly hadn't made any impression on her.

"Hi, Murray."

"I hope I'm not disturbing you, Wanda-Jean."

"No, no. Not really."

He was inside the apartment. He was medium height, clean shaven, and slightly overweight. If her nose didn't deceive her, he was wearing Klein's Bushido. He was dressed in one of those Tokyo designer lounging suits with the drooping hapi shoulders. His only jewelry was a heavy corporation club ring. His face was the kind that fitted—smooth, well proportioned, and unmarked by extremes of either stress or emotion. It fitted so well, in fact, that there was absolutely nothing remarkable about it, nothing to remember it by.

They both stood awkwardly in the middle of Wanda-Jean's small living room.

"Can I get you a drink?"

Murray Dorfman glanced around. "That would be nice."

"Scotch?"

"That'd be fine."

Wanda-Jean was relieved. Scotch was all she had. Unfortunately even her single bottle of Scotch might not prove acceptable—Ashai White Label, only one step above generic. This guy seemed to be well up the status ladder and probably expected Glen something or other.

"Freaz?"

"Sure."

That was another hook she was off. Anyone who took Freaz in their drink wasn't exactly a connoisseur. The splash of the supercold aerosol made a drink taste of nothing but cold without the dilution of ice. Scotch, Freaz, and a sugar cube was the hot drink around the boom-boom bars at the moment.

"Sugar cube?"

"Not for me, I'm sweet enough already."

Wanda-Jean winced. She started to wonder if Murray Dorfman was nothing but an asshole in a good suit. When she came back with a glass in each hand, he was still looking around the room. She nodded to the couch. "Why don't we sit down?"

He made Wanda-Jean tense. She hated the kind of guy who gave her home the hard scrutiny. It invaded too much of her costly privacy.

He sank down onto the couch. Wanda-Jean handed him his drink. She noticed that as he sat down, he carefully pulled up the knees of his pants so the draped silk wouldn't wrinkle.

Wanda-Jean took the armchair. Side by side on the couch would be a lot later, if at all. She tucked one foot under her and watched him take the first sip of his drink. His expression gave no indication that he realized just how rotten the booze was. Either the intense cold of the Freaz hid a multitude of sins, or he didn't know Scotch from shinola.

"So, Murray, what's this all about?"

Murray smiled blandly. "Well, being what you might call Mr. Priest's strong right arm, I thought maybe we should have a little talk."

Anxiety coursed through Wanda-Jean. "Everything's okay, isn't it?"

"Okay?"

"I mean, I'm still on the show, aren't I? I did get through the audition and everything, didn't I?"

Murray laughed. "Yes, of course. That's okay. You've got to realize, though, getting on the show is only the start."

"You have to go on and win. Even I know that."

Murray's smile became somewhat superior. "It's not as easy as that."

"I never imagined it was easy. I found that out at the audition."

"There are ways that it could be made a little easier for special players."

Wanda-Jean didn't like the way the conversation was going, but she kept it to herself. She made her eyes round and innocent. "You're not saying that the games can be fixed?"

Murray made a hasty gesture. "No, no, I'm not saying that at all. There's nothing dishonest about 'Wildest Dreams.' "

"So what are you talking about?"

Murray smiled and leaned back in his seat. He spread his legs so Wanda-Jean was presented with a clear display of the tight material that covered his crotch. "You ever heard the expression 'an inside track'?"

"No."

"It means that some players, selected players, can get a slight edge. It's not a fix, it's just a technique we use to build a more entertaining show."

Wanda-Jean felt a slight chill grab at her. This was the pitch. It was dirty, but there was no way around it. She asked the obvious question. "And which players get this edge?"

"The attractive ones. The ones who really want to win badly enough."

"You think I'm attractive?"

"Very attractive."

"You're pretty nice yourself."

"That's good."

"Is it?"

"Oh, yeah, it really helps if a player's a special friend of one of us who put the show together."

That was it. Wanda-Jean's mind clicked over at high speed. She loathed creeps who didn't have the confidence to get laid on their own account, the ones who thought they had either to bribe you, blackmail you, or get you so stoned that you didn't notice. Shit, he wasn't even bad-looking, she'd have picked him up on a slow night. It was his attitude she objected to. He probably didn't swing all that much muscle on the show. He was more likely to be Bobby Priest's gofer than his right arm. She doubted that there was all that much that he could do for her. On the other hand, if she didn't come across, he probably had enough clout to spoil it for her.

Wanda-Jean made up her mind. She had fucked guys who didn't appeal to her just because she was bored, or she didn't want to be on her own. At least if she fucked this creep it might do her some kind of good.

She smiled and looked at the creep from under her eyelashes. "It'd be good to be someone's special friend."

"You could be mine."

Wanda-Jean put on her best provocative smile. "Really?"

"Really."

She slid out of the chair, letting the kimono fall open slightly. She moved to the floor by Murray's feet. She put a hand on the inside of his thigh. "I think I'd like to be your special friend, Murray."

Her hand made its way up his leg. Her fingers went to work on the zip of his pants. She slipped her hand inside. As she began to manipulate him, she glanced up. Murray's eyes were closed. She stuck out her tongue and

pulled a face. Then she inclined her head and went down
on him.

HE WAS A VIOLENT, THRUSTING GIANT,
little short of a monster, plunging into the girl
beneath him, giving loud animal cries of passion. His whole being was centered on the uncontrollable
power in his loins. The girl rose to meet him, squirming
sinuously, her head rolling from side to side, her black
hair matted with sweat. Her arms twined desperately
around him like urgent seeking snakes. Her nails drew
blood from his back. She too cried and moaned as her
legs gripped his waist and her sharp white teeth sank into
his shoulder.

The power mounted inside him going further and further beyond control and even past the point that he could
bear. The threatening explosion rolled nearer and nearer
like thunderheads born on a barbaric wind. The girl
thrashed about on the hard ground with even greater fe-
rocity.

And finally he came. He burst with a tearing, throb-
bing cry. The girl also screamed, arching her back as
though her spine was going to crack. For long seconds
they clung to each other in rigid tension, then, bit by bit,
it ebbed away. They sank down, hot sweating flesh
pressed against hot sweating flesh. Their limbs tangled
together.

With slow leaden movements he disengaged himself.
The girl made small soft noises, but he ignored her. He
rose to his feet and, drawing himself up to his full height,
he raised his arms to the black sky, the pale moon, and

the cold stars. His lips parted and a high scream of defiance was drawn from him.

The scream echoed off the dolmens of the stone circle and out across the ancient lake. Even the shamans broke off in their ritual torture of the princess. The circle of ghost girls halted their dance and came toward him. Their pale hands reached out. Their cold, dead fingers touched his skin. He shuddered as the living warmth seemed to be drawn out of him.

The stars above him whirled faster and faster. The scene around him grew dim. The power within him failed. It ebbed away and everything became dark. For a terrible instant he was absolutely alone in silent, empty darkness.

There were noises around him. A light shone into his face. He tried to blink it away. Hands were gently lifting him into a sitting position. A woman's face swam into his blurred vision.

"You'll feel just fine in a moment, Mr. Flynn. Just drink this."

A container of hot liquid was placed in his hands. Flynn was back in the real world.

"How did you enjoy Savage Ceremony VI, Mr. Flynn?"

RALPH MOVED WITH THE HEAVY-footed, less than steady stealth of the near drunk. His vision had the crystal clarity that comes at the point when focus is all but lost. One more belt from the bottle and it would be all gone. Ralph, however, hadn't had that belt yet.

Ralph was creeping up on Sam. He had been off on the other side of the vault section, drinking by himself. He had heard Sam talking. Sam had gone on and on talking. Ralph had become partly irked and partly curious. He had decided to creep up on Sam and find out what was happening.

Ralph turned the corner of the row from where Sam's voice was coming. Sam was standing up. That in itself was quite a surprise to Ralph. Sam was usually too tranquilized to stay on his feet for any long space of time. That wasn't the only surprise, though. Sam was staring into the clear plastic cover of one of the cabinets. His face was animated by anxiety. His tone was pleading. Every few seconds he twisted his fat hands together in gestures of extreme frustration.

"How come you got to lie there like that? You must have had so much. You're beautiful and all, and you must have been rich. I mean, you know . . . You could have had it made on the outside. What you want to be lying down here for? You ain't no slob like me. Now me, I couldn't do no better than this, but you . . . You got all the things you could . . ."

"What the hell do you think you're doing?"

Sam swung around. Guilt froze his face. He slowly turned a deep crimson. "Unh . . ."

"Have you gone quite crazy?"

"I . . . er . . ."

Ralph advanced quickly on Sam and grabbed him by the front of his overalls. "You're babbling to a fucking stiff!"

Sam's face was still bright red, but as soon as Ralph took hold of him the flush seemed to take on a different meaning. Ralph was about to make a crack on the lines of Sam getting like Artie when he abruptly changed his mind. An instant flash of drunken insight took in Sam's florid face and whitening knuckles. Ralph quickly let go of him and took a step back.

Sam glowered at him. "I don't like for you to be touching me that way, Ralph."

Ralph took another pace backward and bit his lip. He didn't like the look of this transformed Sam. He wished he were still across the other side of the section, sucking on his bottle. He looked down at the cabinet Sam had been talking to.

"Jesus Christ." The exclamation came out before he could stop it.

Sam glared at him. "What?"

Ralph tried to keep his voice as even as possible. "That's the new stiff, Sam. The one they just brought in."

"So?"

"But why the hell are you talking to her?"

"I like her, Ralph. She's so beautiful, and I feel sorry for her."

Ralph felt a pressure inside his head. It was his turn to make frustrated gestures. "Listen, Sam . . ."

"I don't want to listen, Ralph."

"But she's a stiff."

"I like her, Ralph."

"But she doesn't even know she's here. In her brain she's somewhere else totally."

"I think I'm in love with her, Ralph."

Ralph opened his mouth, and then closed it again. He was about to tell Sam that he was crazy. Instead, he decided to keep quiet. In Sam's present mood, he was just as likely to tear Ralph's head off.

Sam was still looking at him belligerently. "Don't you have nothing to say about that, Ralph?"

Ralph shook his head. "Nothing. Except . . ."

"Except what, Ralph?"

"It's nothing."

"Except what, Ralph?"

Ralph edged away a little more. "I don't want you to get me wrong, Sam."

"Say it, Ralph."

"Well . . . I mean, you wouldn't do anything dumb, would you, Sam?"

"Dumb?"

"You wouldn't do nothing like opening up the cabinet? You wouldn't do nothing like that, would you, Sam?"

Sam gave him a long, hard look. "I think I'd kill anyone who tried to open her up, Ralph. I'm telling you. I think I'd kill anyone who tried to do that."

Ralph dropped his gaze to the floor. He took a deep breath. It required a good deal of effort to keep his voice calm and steady. "Sam."

"What?"

"Sam, I'm going to take myself off."

"Yeah?"

"I'm going to go away across to the other side of the section and go on drinking. I'm going to leave you to get on with whatever you're doing."

Sam nodded. "Okay, Ralph."

Ralph walked slowly away. Now and again he glanced back; Sam was once again talking to the girl in the cabinet, although his gestures were a lot less agitated. Ralph wondered if he had maybe taken a couple of Serenax.

Ralph reached the spot where his bottle was stashed. He sank down on the floor and unscrewed the cap. He took a liberal hit. The heat of the cheap whiskey hit his gut and his brain staggered slightly. He began to feel resentful. There was no doubt about it. He was getting a bum deal. Who needed to be stuck in a situation like the one he was in? First there was a fucking pervert like Artie shulking about, never showing his face and more than likely messing around with the stiffs. Ralph was sure that sooner or later trouble would come down on account of Artie. When it did, he knew the shit wouldn't just stop at him. Some of it would be sure to rub off on Ralph.

Then there was Sam. Sam may have been a pain in the

ass, but he was at least reliable, in his own dumb way. He was always there when he was needed. That, however, was before he had decided to fall in love with the girl stiff. Bitterness, resentment, and disgust knotted in Ralph's throat. He compulsively took another drink. He needed it to stop himself choking. He looked across the orderly, silent rows of the feelie cabinets, each one with its scarcely living stiff.

The bitterness grew stronger and stronger inside Ralph. Those bastards had the right idea—they had gotten the hell out of the whole stinking world. The dirty rich bastards had the whole thing sewn up. They could escape. Ralph and people like him would have to stick with the entire filthy real world until they died and rotted. Ralph was strongly tempted to give it all up: leave the vault, leave the stiffs, and, above all, leave his two crazy partners before he got to be just like them. He ought to just up and quit, go on welfare. He would be just as well off being a wino.

The voices that lurked in the vaults seemed to laugh back at him. Ralph staggered to his feet. He swung around brandishing his bottle as though he was going to take on the whole of the vault.

"Fuck you all! Fuck every one of you!"

Tears sprang into the corners of his eyes. His hands went limp, the bottle fell to the floor. It bounced on the concrete but didn't break. Ralph was stooping to pick it up when the phone went. Ralph ignored it. He carefully set the bottle upright. The phone went on ringing. Ralph checked his bottle from all three sides. The phone still went on ringing. Ralph finally relented. He lurched to the pillar and picked it up.

"Yeah?"

"You took your time."

"So?"

"You all asleep down there?"

"We ain't asleep. What do you want?"

"Just a routine check. Everything okay down there?"

For an instant, Ralph was tempted to tell them all about Sam and Artie and how they were both stone crazy. The instant didn't last too long, though. Ralph suddenly thought, what the hell, they would only send two more mutants. They could be even worse.

"Sure everything's alright. What's with this routine check shit? We never had no routine checks before."

Ralph's belligerence got a mirror response from the other end of the phone.

"Don't take an attitude with me, Mac. It's a new policy order."

"Yeah, sure."

Ralph hung up.

 "PLEASE TELL ME YOUR NAME."

"Frank Zola."

"Please sit down, Frank."

It was one of those intimate HAL 9000 voices, soft, dependable, and reassuring, but, at the same time, strangely dead. Frank sat down. There was just one chair in the viewing pod.

"Relax, Frank."

Frank slid down in the chair a little, but he could not relax. The viewing pods in the basement of the CM building were like tiny individual spaceships, or maybe coffins. Once the airtight door had sighed closed behind him he was alone with just the high-backed contour chair with the speakers built into the headrest and the sixty-inch, high-resolution screen. Although they were used by executives to look at the roughcuts of commercials, view normal tapes, and watch electronic presentations, their unique design was primarily for experiencing audio-visual-chemical mock-ups of feelie software that were complete apart from the Direct Neural Interface itself. They were also used for indoctrination of the newly hired.

"You have joined the family of Combined Media, Frank, and we all hope that you'll be very happy here. Before you commence your duties as a trainee project manager in the public relations department, you and I are going to have a little chat while I show you a short film. You should look on this as a part of the process of your getting acquainted with the corporation."

The screen was a friendly neutral blue. Frank Zola's nose twitched as though a sneeze were starting to build. Frank might have been the new kid in the corporation, the lowliest of the lowly and at the absolute bottom of the ladder, but he wasn't completely innocent. He knew that the corporate ethical philosophy allowed any trick that might be applicable. If CM believed that raining him with a fine mist of chemical softeners pumped in through the air-conditioning vents would aid the induction process, then it would be done. If he was going to get on in the corporation, he knew that he was expected to give them not only his time and service but also his mind. Frank Zola intended to do just that. He wasn't going to complain. He would take whatever they handed out, and he would go on taking it until he was finally in a sufficiently elevated position to be the one who dished it out, and then the poor bastards underneath him would have to watch out.

On the screen, an orchid slowly unfurled against a black background, and the voice was soft and insinuating.

"To grow in the field of public relations is to realize that persuasion is a matter of gentle motion."

The orchid was replaced by a green hillside covered by contentedly grazing white sheep.

"The public doesn't like to be disturbed. Force can only be applied in the most extreme of situations. The keyword is ease. We don't bully—the public will only panic and back away. We don't harangue—they will simply tune us out. We ease. At this moment, and in the immediate foreseeable future, the primary task of the public relations department of this corporation is to ease the public into a full and total acceptance of IE as a part of their lives. In many cases, it will actually become their lives."

The images were speeding up. Well-dressed people thronged a city street during the rush hour; a golden couple made love on silver satin sheets; a perfect blue sphere dropped in slow motion into mirrorlike blue liquid, there was an eruption of the initial splash, and the ripples slowly spread in even, concentric circles. The CM logo shone like the sun.

"We are dealing with a new medium, a medium that has to be handled with tact and diplomacy. If simply thrust at the public it could produce fear and confusion, even guilt."

A blood-red sun set over the skyscrapers of a city. Members of the underclass rioted against a background of burning buildings. Angry music swelled; Nazis marched down a wide boulevard.

"There will be no confusion."

The CM logo no longer glowed like the sun. It was cold, polished steel and white light.

"It has been said more than once that the history of mankind and the cornerstone of our civilization is communication. In the civilization that we are building, communication is everything. We communicate, and the public responds."

The CM logo expanded and spread across an infinite universe in waves of psychedelic color.

"To understand public relations is to understand that it is an infinitely plural art."

Frank Zola was no longer really listening. Something was definitely being pumped into the pod. He stared openmouthed at the images on the screen. He hardly listened to the words. They washed over him, barely touching the conscious leading edge of his mind, sinking instead into the porous depths of his subconscious.

"There are as many answers to a question as there are shades of opinion among the public who are asking it. Our kinship is to the truth, but the relationship is a complex one. In this house, there are many truths, equal but separate. All is never what it appears, and the stages of strategy may not yield the obvious end result. Would you like an example?"

"Y-yes."

Frank Zola found that he was actually nodding, responding to a piece of software.

It was so sudden that it took him completely by surprise. The big close-up was of a construction worker, tanned and smiling in yellow hard hat, blue jeans, and a red plaid workshirt—a total blue-collar stereotype. He grinned into the camera.

"I tell you one thing, buddy, when I get my bonus, I'm going to have me a feelie. Ain't no son of a bitch gonna stop me."

The hard hat image froze. The Hal 9000 voice came back.

"Are you surprised, Frank? We used the word *feelie*. You probably thought we never said that word. Standing Directive 1341 stipulates that the word 'cheapens and degrades the image of the IE service and will, under no circumstances, be used in a public context.' You'll probably be even more surprised to learn that the word was made up right here in PR. The word *feelie* is our gift to the people. It is the common colloquial term. It's not our word—it's their word. *IE* belongs to the corporation, but *feelie* is the property of the people."

The screen showed hundreds of stereotyped workers

marching across a vast flat expanse, rank behind rank, all the way to the horizon. It had to be a computer simulation. Heroic music began to swell under the voice.

"It's the people's word, Frank. It's something that belongs to them. It's their ultimate hope. It's the machine that can solve all their problems."

The CM logo was back, but this time it was hewn from black stone, dark and forbidding, a brooding monolith that cast a long dark shadow over the marching workers. The Hal 9000 voice was mournful.

"The people don't like the corporation, Frank. They don't like us at all. We are the only thing that stands between them and the fulfillment of their fantasies. The corporation is the bogeyman. It set up the price system that limits the service to the wealthy. It is the corporation that excludes the poor and the underclass. They hate us, but we don't mind. We understand, and we forgive. We know what is best, and we will do what is best even if cruelty is the only route to the ultimate kindness. It is better they resent the corporation than feel that the service was something being inflicted on them. This way they want the service, Frank. And they believe that it's their own idea that they want it. And it doesn't stop at wanting. They covet it; they yearn for it. They'd go into debt or steal for it if they thought that would bring it within their reach."

The voice suddenly hardened. "Anything that will one day be the ultimate means of confining the excess population of this planet has to be something that the excess population desires with all its collective being. That's public relations, Frank."

The CM logo was back, proud as an eagle. The flag was behind it. The background music wasn't quite the national anthem, but it came very close. Tears streamed down Frank Zola's face. A small part of his mind kept telling him that it was all chemical softeners and bullshit, that what the computer had been saying to him was knee-jerk nonsense, but he couldn't help himself. Waves of powerful if patently phony emotion were coursing through him like deep gasping shudders—and the voice still wasn't through with him.

"Listen to me carefully, Frank. Listen to me. The IE is the machine that will solve the world's problem. *Solve* is an anagram of *loves*, Frank. Did you hear that? *Solve* is an anagram of *loves*, Frank. In public relations, Frank, we have to love the public. Our power is based only in love, Frank. We love every last one of them."

Frank was nodding helplessly. He wanted to love the public. He wanted the power to love the public. He wanted the power of love. He wanted the power. He wanted the power to love the bastards right to death.

"In the next few months, Frank, we will have more of these little chats. They are a crucial part of the indoctrination process. In thirty seconds, the pod door will open. Please leave quickly and quietly."

WANDA-JEAN WAS STARTING TO GET TO know some of the other regular contestants. There was the hostile girl with dark hair called Sylvia; Danny, the long-haired kid from some small town who seemed to train all the time; Paul, the blond boy who kept himself to himself; and Nancy, who came on real friendly, but who was probably more of a ruthless gouger than any of them.

The five of them were kind of thrown together. The competition was too intense on any game show for the players ever to form proper friendships. The only reason these five knew one another's names was because they

were all at the same level on the show. They had all
survived their initial appearances, and had one more show
to go before they could get on the Dreamroad.

Of course, by the time they reached the Dreamroad,
there would no longer be five of them. At the most, two
might have come through, more probably it would be
one, or maybe they would all go down during the next
screening.

Wanda-Jean knew a few more of the contestants by
sight. They were the ones who had come onto the show
after her. The mere fact of getting through two programs
unscathed made her a veteran already.

And, of course, there was Ramone, the dark, faggy
field leader who was almost at the end of the Dreamroad.
Not that she spoke or even got close to Ramone. The
network had him stashed away in a top downtown hotel.
He was constantly guarded so no one could interfere with
him. There was a buzz, however, that Ramone wouldn't
make it through to a feelie contract. Behind the scenes
rumor had him going down to Suzie, the vacant-looking
farm girl, in the very next show. Wanda-Jean had learned
that behind the scenes rumor was uncannily accurate.

Wanda-Jean had learned a great deal during her short
time on "Wildest Dreams." Most of it didn't do much
to make her any happier about the life she was living.
One of the first things she had discovered was that fucking Murray wasn't going to do a damn thing for her. As
she had suspected at the very beginning, Murray was far
from being Bobby Priest's right hand. He was a gofer,
and a pretty low-level gofer, at that. She had compared
notes with some of the other girls. It turned out that he
pulled the same stunt on just about every personable female who passed the audition. The most galling part was
that his bullshit usually worked.

Murray Dorfman's proposition wasn't the last of that
kind, either. As Wanda-Jean moved closer toward the
Dreamroad, the offers simply came from higher up the

studio hierarchy. All Wanda-Jean could do was to become more selective as she progressed through the show. She still couldn't afford to upset anyone who mattered. There was too much at stake.

Wanda-Jean knew she ought to have been happy. With two shows under her belt she was turning into a minor celebrity. Her name had appeared in one of the game show gossip sheets. Her phone rang all the time. Old boyfriends, whom she hadn't seen in months, suddenly remembered how desirable she was and wanted to date her. Again, she had to learn to be selective.

The most surprising part was the way that total strangers yelled at her in the street. Some wished her luck, others made smutty comments. They treated her as though they knew her intimately. It was as if she had become part of their lives.

Wanda-Jean ought to have been reveling in it all. It was a way of life that she had always dreamed about. For the first time in her life, she was somebody. Admittedly she was only a minor somebody, not a star like Bobby Priest or Fay Fox from "The Torture Garden," but a somebody all the same.

There was a problem, however. It just wasn't the way she had imagined it. Something was wrong. She wasn't sleeping at nights. She was drinking more and feeding herself a whole lot more pills. At first she thought it might have been the procession of Murrays who came knocking on her door, with their eager, smooth faces and busy, clammy hands. She dismissed that theory. She could handle the Murrays. Christ, she'd been handling them, to one degree or another, all her life.

She also found she could handle the way the show was specifically set up to degrade the players. So she got knocked down and pushed around, so the animals in the crowd yelled abuse at her, so she generally ended each game bare-ass naked. She found that as long as she was winning she could almost take a perverse pleasure in what they put her through.

"As long as she was winning" seemed to be the key phrase. The thing that stopped her enjoying her new-found fame was exactly that. She only had to foul up once and it would be all over. A single mistake and she'd be nobody again, just like that. There was a current of tension that ran through every aspect of her new life. It made it impossible for her to relax. Even if she got through to the Dreamroad, it would only get worse.

Wanda-Jean knew she ought to be looking forward to the Dreamroad. The idea of the downtown hotel, the crowds that would gather outside the hotel or the studios just to stare at her, and the bodyguards in constant atten-dance should have been the experience of a lifetime, something to wait for with bated breath. As it came closer, however, it just didn't feel right. She was starting to view the whole thing with extreme trepidation.

She even felt guilty about her doubts and fears. She knew that she wasn't reacting in the right way. There were millions of people who'd give their right arms to be in her place. It didn't seem fair. How could you possibly enjoy anything that came neatly packaged with a constant reminder that it was likely to be taken away in an instant?

Wanda-Jean's train of thought was cut off and jerked back to earth by the ringing of the phone. At first she ignored it. There were a lot of phone calls since she'd appeared on TV. Most of them wanted something, fre-quently her body.

It went on ringing. Despite her state of mind Wanda-Jean had never had what it takes to sit by a ringing phone. By the time it had rung seven times, Wanda-Jean's will-power crumbled. She picked it up.

"Hello."

"This is building security," a female robot voice said.

Wanda-Jean sighed. "I don't want to see anyone."

"A letter has arrived for you. It came Fedex."

Wanda-Jean's heart stopped. The letter had to be about the next game. The specifics were sent to each contestant on the day before the taping of each show. The letter would tell her exactly which obstacle course she had drawn.

"I'll come down and get it."

"Your letter is with the duty doorman. Please hold the line. He will be with you momentarily."

There was a brief burst of easy-listening hold music.

"Hello, Wanda-Jean, this is Reuben."

Reuben was one of the token human doormen. He was a tiny birdlike Hispanic with a scarcely concealed drinking problem.

"Yeah . . . uh . . . listen, Reuben, I'll be right down to pick it up."

"I'll bring it up if you like."

"You would?"

"Sure. No trouble."

"Hey, thanks."

"I'll be up right away."

Wanda-Jean hung up. From where she sat, she could see out of the apartment window. There was really nothing to look at. Only the smog and the identical apartment building across the street. It suddenly seemed to her that Reuben was about the only person she could trust. A doorman was the only person she could count on. She knew she ought to take some pills and snap out of this mood. It was probably only a comedown.

The door buzzed. Wanda-Jean got up to answer it. As she had expected, it was Reuben. Reuben wasn't the most impressive figure of a man Wanda-Jean had ever seen. He was a good two inches shorter than her. The pale gray uniform provided by the owners of the building was about two sizes too large.

He had the familiar white envelope with him. He held it out to Wanda-Jean, but she didn't take it. Suddenly she didn't want to be alone when she opened the message from the show.

"Why don't you come inside for a moment, Reuben?"

Reuben hesitated. "I didn't ought to be away from the door for too long. There ain't no one to cover for me."

"A few minutes won't make all that much difference."

Reuben reluctantly came inside. Wanda-Jean went over to the liquor cabinet.

"You want a drink?"

"I . . ."

"Sure you want a drink. Why don't you sit down?"

Reuben settled uncomfortably on the very edge of an easy chair that was solely designed to be lounged in. His uniform threatened to drown him. Wanda-Jean mixed the drinks. One of the compensations of being on "Wildest Dreams" was that she could now afford Scotch from Scotland. She handed Reuben a drink.

"You look in a sorry state."

Reuben raised an eyebrow. "You don't look exactly on top of things yourself."

Wanda-Jean laughed. Somehow she couldn't stop the laugh coming out brittle. "I don't?"

"Not for a big game-show star."

Wanda-Jean sighed. "Don't even talk about it."

"It's getting to you."

Reuben was still holding the envelope. He held it out. "Aren't you going to open this?"

Wanda-Jean still didn't take it.

Reuben turned it over between his fingers. "You want I should open it for you?"

"Would you?"

"Sure."

Reuben quickly slit open the envelope. The icy chill grabbed Wanda-Jean's gut with a vengeance.

"Read it to me. Which game is it?"

Reuben scanned the single sheet of crisp, expensive notepaper. "They've put you on Personality Fall Down."

"Jesus Christ!"

"It's not that bad."

"It's the worst. I'll never get through that."

"Sure you will."

Wanda-Jean sagged into a chair. She looked a picture of misery.

"It's really nice of you to try and encourage me, Reuben, but this has got to be the end for me."

Wanda-Jean had seen Personality Fall Down enough times to convince herself that she didn't have a chance. It was a game where the contestants stood in glass booths. Under the booths was a tank of liquid mud. Rapid general knowledge questions were fired at you. If you didn't keep getting them right, the floor of the booth slowly opened and you dropped through into the mud.

Wanda-Jean could picture the scene all too vividly. The crowd would be baying and screaming as she dragged herself out of the mud and into oblivion. At least she'd be spared the Dreamroad, and the torture of knowing that the behind the scenes gossip was busily predicting her fall. She would have taken her fall already.

Reuben put his half-finished drink down on the floor. He began to get up. Wanda-Jean started in panic. Was even Reuben going to desert her?

"You haven't finished your drink yet."

Reuben looked unhappy. "I got to get back to work. I really only took time out to bring that letter up to you. I figured you'd want it straightaway."

"You sure you won't stay? At least finish your drink."

"I really got to go."

Wanda-Jean arranged herself in the chair so she would look as appealing as possible. "Don't go yet."

Reuben was almost at the door. He half turned. For a moment their eyes met. Then Reuben looked away. His voice was soft and regretful.

"I can't do what you want, Wanda-Jean."

Before Wanda-Jean could work out what he meant, he had let himself quietly out of the flat.

For a long time, Wanda-Jean sat staring at the door. Her depression had gone past rational thought and descended into a morose blankness. The phone rang again. Wanda-Jean absently picked it up. It was a reflex action.

"Yeah?"

"Hi, is that Wanda-Jean?"

The voice was gratingly enthusiastic and friendly. Wanda-Jean's was correspondingly dull and flat.

"This is she, who's that?"

"It's Charlie, honey. You remember, don't you?"

"No."

"Oh, come on now. Good old Charlie. Hell, we had one great night after . . ."

Wanda-Jean hung up and cried.

THERE HAD TO BE A WAY OUT. THERE just had to be.

The sound of boots rang from somewhere at the other end of the corridor. They were coming. Christopher Elwin III never knew when they were going to come. The schedules were constantly being altered, and the prisoners were kept permanently guessing. It was all part of the general policy of psychological disorientation. Christopher Elwin III's conditioned instinct was to do something, to sit bolt upright, to scan the cell for any little thing out of place, any blemish on the code of absolute spotlessness. Unfortunately, Christopher Elwin III wasn't able to do anything. Christopher Elwin could hardly move a muscle. He and the female prisoner lay pressed together, face to face on the hard, narrow bunk. Leather straps held them secured together at the wrists and ankles. Their collars were joined at the neck, and a wide leather belt was cinched tightly around both their waists. Her breasts were squeezed against his chest, her stomach and thighs were pressed against his, and the two of them were completely helpless. While Major Freda, the section commandant, had looked on with that cold, cruel smile of hers, Inga and Greta, the daytime guards on their tier, had bound them in that position before lights out, and they had been left that way all night. Close as he was to her, he didn't even know the woman's name. When she had been brought into the cell, they had only referred to her as Female Prisoner #27, just as he was always called Male Prisoner #19. The final orders had been simple.

"No talking."

"No sex."

There was no room for misunderstanding. The slightest attempt at either would result in the most severe of punishments. There was also no deceiving the guards. All through the sleepless, muscle-cramping night they had been relentlessly observed by the black lens of the cell's surveillance camera. A whispered word or the slightest movement would be instantly noticed as well as recorded on tape for later disciplinary review. One of the favorite tricks of the guards was to force prisoners to watch tapes of their transgressions while physical correction was being inflicted on them. Rumors circulated throughout the prison of edited versions of these tapes, along with tapes of the punishments and executions, being circulated on the black market for the amusement and titillation of the party matriarchs and ranking officers of the secret police.

The boots were coming nearer. The flesh of Christopher Elwin III actually started to crawl in anticipation of what might happen when the guards reached his cell. He guessed that Female Prisoner #27 was going through a

similar spasm of scared anticipation. Risking the wrath
of the video camera, she silently rolled her eyes. Then
the boots stopped. An order was barked. It was Greta's
voice.

"Open cell thirteen."

There was the grinding of metal on metal as the door
to cell thirteen was cranked open. Male Prisoner #13 was
in trouble. Inga and Greta must have spotted something
amiss in his cell, or maybe something had shown up on
the overnight videotapes. Male Prisoner #13 was uncom-
monly unlucky.

Greta's voice barked again. "You are a filthy, disgusting little worm, Number Thirteen. I don't think I can
imagine a filthier, more disgusting little worm than you."

#13 muttered something that Christopher Elwin III
couldn't quite make out. Greta responded with anger and
outrage.

"Did I tell you to speak? Get down on your knees,
right now!"

There were more mutterings, #13's tone abject and
pleading.

Greta was not moved. "Shut your filthy mouth. You're
only making it worse for yourself."

Christopher Elwin III could all too easily imagine what
#13 was going through. He had been through it himself
more times than he would ever want to remember. He
was all-too familiar with the experience of crouching on
the floor of his cell, on eye level with the highly polished
boots of the two guards, glancing furtively up at the two
statuesque blondes standing over him with their long legs,
tight black uniform shirts, starched white shirts, black
ties, and triple star Arena Party armbands.

There was a sharp swish and the slap of leather hitting
flesh. #13 whimpered. The majority of the female guards
carried canes when they were on the cell block, Greta
was something of an individualist within the narrow con-
fines of the regime. She always had a wicked leather strap

hanging from her wrist and was always ready to wield it with a strong-armed will if a prisoner displeased her. There was another swish and another slap. #13 whimpered again. The sequence was repeated a good twenty times.

"On your feet, worm. Stop groveling on the floor. Go and stand facing the corner. That's right, face to the wall. Now you will remain there until otherwise ordered."

The boots moved out of cell thirteen. The barred door ground closed behind them. They were coming on down the corridor. Female Prisoner #27 closed her eyes.

"Open cell nineteen."

The noise of the door sliding back seemed deafening. In moments of tension, sounds always seemed unusually loud. And then the two guards were in the cell looking down at them.

"This is a cozy little scene, isn't it? We trust you lovebirds both slept well."

Christopher Elwin III suppressed a shudder as the tip of Inga's cane lightly traced a pattern down his naked back. He dared not turn his head even slightly to look at his tormentors.

One of the women walked the length of the cell and back again. "This togetherness is all very well, but we can't have you lying around doing nothing all day. You're not here for a holiday."

Black-gloved hands were unfastening the straps on the prisoners' wrists and ankles; then the belt was taken off. Finally the neck chain was removed, though the leather collars, numbered dogtags hanging from them, remained in place.

"Okay, up! On your feet, the both of you!"

Christopher Elwin III winced as he tried to stand straight. He longed to massage his painfully cramped muscles. Circulation came back in an agony of pins and needles. Greta's strap slashed viciously across his thighs.

"Stand up, you scum! At attention! You want a dose of what Number Thirteen got?"

She glared into his face. Christopher Elwin III turned his gaze downward to the floor. It wasn't a good idea to look the guards directly in the eye.

"No, madam."

"Louder, maggot, I can't hear you!"

Christopher Elwin III stiffened his shoulders and raised his voice, but he didn't lift his eyes from the floor. "No, madam. I don't want what Number Thirteen got, madam."

"And what did he get?"

"Madam, he got a beating, madam."

"You think he deserved it, maggot?"

"I know he deserved it, madam. We always deserve our punishments."

The exchange seemed to satisfy Greta. She and Inga turned their attention to Female Prisoner #27.

"So how did you enjoy your night next to a man, slut? I'd imagine a promiscuous little whore like you would do anything to get next to a man, even a pathetic specimen like this."

It was one of those questions that was almost impossible to answer without the risk of an instant beating. #27 did the best she could.

"Madam, I wasn't ordered to enjoy the experience."

It was a clever answer, but it bordered on being too clever. Greta took off her mirrored aviator glasses. Her eyes were hard.

"Think you're pretty smart, don't you, slut?"

#27 had turned pale. "No, madam, I'm not smart."

"Outside!"

#27 didn't move quickly enough. The cane lashed out, leaving a red welt across her buttocks.

"Move, slut! Make *schnell*!"

Then Christopher Elwin III was alone with Inga and Greta.

"At attention, worm. First inspection!"

Christopher Elwin III braced himself. Greta's leather-gloved hand reached between his legs.

By that point, Christopher Elwin III should have been in the throes of guilty delight. The S & M prison fantasy was something that had turned him on for all of his adult life. The idea of powerful Germanic women using him, controlling him, subjecting him to ritualized pain had been his obsession for as long as he could remember, and he had spent hundreds of thousands of dollars over the years having prostitutes stage approximations of it. The problem was that it no longer worked. As far as he could calculate—and the relative passage of time was very hard to estimate—he had only been in the feelie for maybe a month, and he wanted out. He was not being constantly filled with breathless cringing excitement. He was not being maintained in a continually heightened state of claustrophobic sexuality. He was merely cringing and claustrophobic. Even though it was an electronically cre-ated illusion, his only reality was life in a very uncom-fortable prison with no chance of parole, constantly at the mercy of a set of brutal psychopaths, beauty notwith-standing, who had been created for him out of his own imagination. Worst of all, he had doomed himself to it for the rest of his life.

The one thing that he had no illusions about was his own value in the real world. He was a loser and that was it, the classic case of ineffectual son of the dynamic fa-ther. Christopher Elwin II had built Elwin Systems into the highly profitable component satellite of a number of major corporations. He, Christopher Elwin III—little Chris was what they had always called him—had all but run it into the ground. The family had done little to con-ceal their relief when he had opted for the big sleep. Now his brother Lance, who seemed to have been the one to inherit their father's smarts, could have a free hand to rebuild the Elwin fortunes.

There was a lot more to the preparation for an IE life-span contract than merely buying a ticket. In his price bracket, the feelie was custom-made to his exact requirements. There had been long sessions with the very over-priced company shrink. "Go with the fantasy," she had told him. "Push it to the limit. We can only supply you with what you give us. You want it to be perfect, don't you?" He had poured out the whole catalog of his grubby imaginings, every disgusting idea that he had reveled in from the age of eleven onward. It had to be the ultimate irony. Now that he had them made real, he didn't like them. There was a part of his mind that was becoming more and more detached from the fantasy, and the more detached it became, the closer it steered toward a state of blind panic. The difficulty was that, inside a feelie, there was no such thing as a panic button. How could he communicate to the outside world that he wanted out? There had to be some way. There just had to be. If he couldn't get free from his own fantasies, his mind was going to come unhinged. There was a definite limit to how much he could take, and that limit was drawing close.

Inga's voice dragged him back into the all-too familiar scenario. The tip of her cane was probing the crack in his ass.

"I hope you're well rested, maggot. The commandant has a party of visitors coming to the facility today, and she wants some prisoners put through their paces for them. The good news is that you're one of the lucky ones who've been selected for the display team."

Christopher Elwin III groaned inwardly. That was an-other problem. In a feelie crafted from his own imaginings, he always knew what was coming. This so-called display would mean a gruelling session of pain and hu-miliation in front of an amused audience. Suppose he fought the program? Surely there had to be something built into the software that would show that he was not responding according to the expected pattern and trigger some kind of alarm. He toyed with the idea of ripping Inga's cane out of her hand and hurling the woman across the cell. To his disappointment, he found that all he could do was follow the expected responses.

"Yes, madam. It will be an honor to perform for the commandant."

The detached part of his mind was dizzy with frustration. There had to be a way out. There just had to be.

 "YEAH, WELL, A LOT OF THEM ARE JUST plain smut."

"Smut?"

"Yeah, smut. Sex. Fucking. Men fucking women, women fucking women, men fucking men. Men, women, children, animals, threes, fours, dozens. You name it, they're doing it. Any number, any variation." Ralph swung his arm in a sweeping if unsteady gesture that took in the whole of the vault. "It's just one huge electronic whorehouse."

Sam blinked twice. "It can't be that bad. Not everybody wants sex all the time."

Ralph sneered. "You think not? I'm telling you. There ain't many stiffs here plugged into the life of Socrates or St. Francis of Assisi, and that's a fact."

Sam took a while to digest all that. Then a puzzled expression wrinkled his doughy features. "What have you got against sex?"

Ralph looked at him impatiently. "Nothing, except I maybe don't get enough."

Sam's voice became morose. "I don't get any . . . except . . ."

Ralph cut him off. "I don't want to hear what you get up to when you're away from here."

It was drawing toward the end of the shift. It was that part of the day when Ralph was drunk belligerent and Sam was little short of comatose. Ralph would rant, and Sam would stare dully into space. It was the point when communication was at a minimum.

In between outbursts, Ralph would sit grim and hunched until he had worked up enough bile for another one. It was during these silences that Sam would throw out the occasional remark.

"Ralph?"

"What?"

"How do you know?"

"How do I know what?"

"How do you know that all they want is sex? You've never been in a feelie."

"I've seen the catalog, haven't I?"

"What catalog?"

"The catalog of all the different feelie experiences that they offer."

"I've never seen that."

"You know when you first sign on they give you a guided tour of one of the reception centers."

Sam looked glum. "They never took me on the tour."

"Why not?"

"I don't know. They just kind of left me behind."

"They left you behind?"

"Yeah."

Ralph hesitated. He seemed about to make some comment. He changed his mind. "Well, anyway. While they were going on about what a great thing the feelies were for humanity, I managed to get a good look at the catalog. That's when I first decided that it was all bullshit."

"I don't think it's bullshit."

Ralph's lip curled. "What do you know about it?"

"I know I'd like to get in a feelie."

"I'm telling you, it's all just sex and violence. It's about the lowest you can get."

Sam inspected his fingers. "Sometimes I think that we're the lowest you can get."

"What?"

"Nothing."

They lapsed into another sullen silence. Sam started playing with the zip on his overall. First he'd pull it down for about six inches, then he would pull it up again. He did it over and over. Ralph watched him. His irritation increased with each run of the zip.

"What the hell do you think you're doing?"

"At least they're quiet."

"Huh?"

"At least they're quiet."

"Who are?"

"The stiffs."

"What the hell are you going on about now?"

"The stiffs, at least they're quiet."

"Of course they're quiet. They're always quiet. They're stiffs. They're quiet by definition."

"I didn't mean that."

"You didn't mean that?"

"No."

Ralph was visibly controlling himself. "So what the hell did you mean?"

"I guess I mean . . . I don't know. I think I've forgotten."

Sam went back to playing with his zip.

"Do you have to do that?"

"It passes the time."

"Like the stiffs, I suppose."

"What?"

"Passing the time."

"Oh . . . yeah."

"You're a great conversationalist."

"I am?"

"Jesus Christ!"

Ralph looked at his watch. There was another hour of the shift still to go. Ralph's bottle was empty, and he wanted another drink. It had to be the worst time of the shift. He got to his feet and paced up and down the row of cabinets. There was a dull ache in the back of his head. After four or five turns along the row, he stopped and stared down at Sam.

"I'm sick of this fucking job."

"It's a job."

"I'd be better off on welfare."

"You wouldn't like it on welfare."

"Why not?"

"I wouldn't like it on welfare. I like to have a job. It gives me some self-respect."

"Self-respect?"

"That's right."

"Listen, what the hell do you know about self-respect?"

"I do the job I'm paid for. That's self-respect."

"You reckon?"

"Yeah."

"You sit around all day and gobble down tranquilizers. That's when you're not staring at the girl in the cabinet like some lovesick calf."

"I don't think that's fair."

"It's true enough."

"Maybe that's what I'm paid for."

"And that's what keeps your precious self-respect together?"

"I suppose so."

"You're weird, Sam."

"No."

"No, what?"

"I don't think I'm weird."

Ralph looked at him in amazement. "You don't?"

"I think I'm pretty average, really."

Ralph closed his eyes with an expression of pain. "Anything you say, Sam."

Ralph went back to pacing. Sam went back to playing with his zip. Ralph looked at his watch again. Fifty-five minutes to go. It had to be the most boring job on God's earth. They could at least give them something to do. If there was some real work to fill the time, he wouldn't have to drink so much, and he wouldn't have to get involved in these pointless conversations with Sam. For the hundredth time, he resolved to throw the whole thing in and take his chances on the street.

Ralph became aware that Sam had stopped fiddling with his overalls and was watching him intently. Ralph swung around and snapped at him. "What's the matter with you now?"

"Nothing."

"You look like you're about to come out with some portentous remark."

"What does portentous mean?"

"Forget it."

"You shouldn't use words like that if you ain't prepared to explain what they mean."

"I just work with you, right? I ain't no teacher."

"You don't have to be like that about it."

"I don't?"

"We might as well try and get along."

Ralph sighed. "Yeah, yeah. Okay."

"I was going to say something."

"You were?"

"Yeah."

Ralph waited, but Sam didn't go on. After about a minute, Ralph couldn't stand it any longer.

"So?"

"So what?"

"So what were you going to say?"

Sam looked dolefully at Ralph. "I don't think you'd be interested."

"You'll probably tell me anyway."

"I don't think I'll bother."

"Oh, Jesus. Get it out."

"I was watching TV last night."

"You watch TV?"

"Of course I watch TV. Everyone watches TV."

"And that's it?"

"I was watching TV last night. There was this show about telepathy."

"You watch the egghead shows?"

"I watch all kinds of things. I like TV."

"So what about telepathy?"

"Well, it seems to me that if we could all read each other's minds we'd get really paranoid."

"We would?"

"Yeah. I mean, it's bad enough having to watch what you say. Just imagine if you had to watch everything you thought."

"I'm imagining."

"Well?"

"Well?"

"It wouldn't be very nice, would it? I think we'd all get very paranoid."

Ralph was a picture of disbelief. "What in God's name does that have to do with anything?"

Sam looked mildly surprised. "Nothing."

"Then why tell me about it?"

"I thought you might be interested."

Ralph clenched his fists. It was only their respective size and weight that stopped him from hitting Sam.

LOMBARDS, JUST ONE BLOCK FROM THE foot of the CM tower, charged top price for its drinks and catered to the executive trade and, as such, was much frequented by the upper ranks of Combined Media employees during the happy hour. It was a place to see and, on occasion, to be seen to see. It was the place where the crucial, postwork, public-display games, both social and corporate political, were played out for an audience who watched for who was with whom under the dim chandeliers and guessed at the rest with varying degrees of accuracy. Department coups had been started in Lombards, and, at the other end of the scale, so had a large number of office romances. The atmosphere of top-shelf booze and cigar smoke was the favorite medium for the sending of signals, the making of overtures, the conclusion of honeymoons, and the termination of alliances and relationships. If one wanted to make career points in CM, it was vital to drop into Lombards at least three or four times a month and show one's face. It was even expected of the militant nondrinkers that they come by for at least a Perrier and twist at regular intervals.

The power positions in Lombards were along the line of leather upholstered banquettes that ran from just inside the front door clear through to the back wall. Seated in the comfort of one of these, a person could observe the action at the bar and the regular tables without being watched or overheard. Pride of place in the entire prestige row was the banquette just to the left of center, slightly nearer the door than the rear wall. On this par-

ticular night, this number one booth was occupied by two
men whose status and rights to the booth would never be
questioned even by the most inexperienced waiter.
Edouard Hayes was the Senior Vice President for Special
Projects. The second man, Jack Vallenti, was the number
two man in the Software Development Division. The fact
that the two of them would place themselves even on
discreet display like this indicated to anyone who read
between the lines that something radical was brewing.
Their respective departments, whose territory tended to
overlap in the area of advance planning, had butted heads
on a number of occasions, and the seemingly casual
meeting for a drink was open to a number of interpreta-
tions. The most popular were the two obvious extremes:
either a truce or the start of a new round of hostilities.

The meeting started as casually as it was supposed to
look. Hayes ordered a martini and Vallenti a Scotch on
the rocks. There was some small talk about how Rostov
in Marketing seemed to be teetering on the brink of making a damn fool of himself over his secretary and how
Madison Renfield had made a damn fool of himself on
"The Bones Bolt Show." When Vallenti brought up the
subject of Renfield, Hayes sadly shook his head.

"Sooner or later somebody's got to stop him. I mean,
what makes that pompous jackass believe that he can be
an adequate spokesperson for the corporation on something as wild and woolly as 'Bones Bolt'?''

Vallenti swirled the ice in his drink. "That's the trouble with PR. They can cover most of their screwups by
claiming that they were working according to some devious, deep-psych program. According to them, they can
never be wrong. It's just that the rest of us don't appreciate the subtlety of what they're doing. We can't see the
big picture."

"It doesn't hurt any that Renfield knows where a hell
of a lot of bodies are buried. He's hushed up a lot of
people's indiscretions in his time, and he's not going to

go quietly when the crunch comes. He'll call in all of his markers, and in public if need be, before he allows himself to be deposed.''

"I hear that he practically brainwashes his new arrivals these days. Weekly indocrinations in the viewing pods downstairs with the chemical softeners going full blast.''

Hayes looked at Vallenti in real amazement. "Sure he does. I thought everyone did. It's hardly the time for loose cannons rolling around or for underlings to be plotting revolution. You mean you don't do that over in Development?''

Vallenti covered his loss of face by signaling for a waiter. They had arrived at the point in the conversation when the two of them should cut out the third-party gossip and get down to business, and he was furious at himself for having reached it at a distinct disadvantage. Why in hell didn't his department brainwash the newly hired? Anything that kept the help loyal and docile had to be in everyone's best interests. When the waiter brought him another Scotch, he turned the subject around to the reason that he had asked Hayes there in the first place.

"So how are you getting along with Project Superstar?''

It was Hayes's turn to look surprised. "You heard about Superstar.''

"Just a whisper.''

"I think I'm going to have to make some inquiries as to who's been whispering in the ranks. This thing's supposed to be fully under wraps.''

Vallenti smiled. They were back on even pegging. Apparently Hayes's brainwashing was not yielding the results for which he had been hoping. Interdepartmental spying was conducted on all levels, but Special Projects took great pride in being among the least pregnable. Vallenti was delighted to have punctured their smug assurance. He gave Hayes a few moments to recover his composure before continuing.

"Those of us in Development who know about this are, to put it mildly, a little worried."

Hayes raised an eyebrow. He still looked a little worried himself. "How many of you know about Superstar?"

Vallenti held up a reassuring hand. "Don't worry, Hayes, it's really just a handful of us. We've totally respected your need for privacy. It's just that we wonder if what you're doing may be, to put it very bluntly, a trifle misdirected."

Hayes's eyes hardened. "I'd like to hear exactly what you think Superstar actually is."

"The way we heard it, you're planning to wire up a major teen hearthrob during a special live show, and that it will be marketed to the fans as a chance actually to be their idol in a special two-hour package deal. It's going to be the spearhead of a number of short-term forays into the youth market."

"You seem to have heard a great deal."

Vallenti grinned. "We don't know who you intend to use as the first subject."

"That's a relief."

"Why don't you lift the corner of the dustsheet and let me in on the secret?"

Hayes shook his head. "I can't do that. The deal isn't finalized yet and we really can't afford anyone else knowing. Why don't you just tell me what's bothering you all over at Development? What is it about this project that you think is so misdirected?"

Vallenti sipped his Scotch. "To be frank, we have never done particularly well with live recordings of any kind. God knows we tried for long enough. The clients just won't accept reality. It's too damned flat. The computer composites are quite literally a hundred times better."

"I think you're rather missing the point."

"You're telling me that I'm not seeing the big picture?"

"If you like."

Vallenti scowled. "Now you're sounding like Renfield."

"We're not going to market just the live recording. We'll make a tape of this entertainer, but then it will be subjected to all the same processing as any simulated fantasy. Even in those, you do have to use recorded experiences as base material." Hayes grinned. "I mean, where else would you get your orgasms except from a tape of the real thing?"

"So the live experience angle is really just a marketing ploy. You're really paying a fortune to have this guy's name on the advertising. Basically it's very much the same as the Elvis Presley or Michael Jackson experiences that we already have on catalog."

"Except that this guy is alive and current and topping the Billboard chart."

Vallenti laughed. "So the subject is male?"

Hayes grimaced at his slip. "I guess that narrows the field for you by half."

Vallenti suddenly leaned forward. He wasn't laughing anymore. It was time to drop the bomb on Hayes—the bomb that was the real point of the meeting. "You want to know what else is bothering us about Project Superstar?"

Hayes looked at Vallenti suspiciously. "I somehow thought that your major concern wasn't that our efforts might fail."

"Are you sure that this whole thing isn't a cover for clandestine work on a death-experience program?"

Hayes's eyes widened. "A death-experience program? Are you joking?"

Either Hayes was genuinely shocked, or he was a consummate actor. Vallenti shook his head.

"I'm not joking. The information is that death-

experience research has been resumed. You have to admit
that your project would be an ideal cover.''

"But work on the death experience is strictly forbidden
after what Jonas did. You know that as well as I do. His
attempts to tape through a human death nearly ruined
us.''

"Someone's messing around with it again.''

"It's no one in Special Projects. I can assure you of
that.''

"Can you be certain?''

"It's my department, damn it. And how can you be so
sure anyway?''

"We have evidence.''

"What evidence?''

"Supply requisitions.''

"How can they prove anything on their own? We've
booked out truckloads of live recording gear for the research on Superstar.''

"That's what made us think it might be you guys.''

"I already told you. It wasn't us.''

"There is one other piece of evidence.''

"I think I need another martini.''

"Three weeks ago there was a execution down in Mississippi. A character by the name of Jamal Vance. He
killed five people when a supermarket heist turned sour.''

"What about him?''

"We have a tape and polygraph record of a prison
guard who claims to have, along with three others, sub-
stituted a gimmicked execution gurney that was capable
of recording Vance's feelings from the moment that he
was strapped down to it, through the lethal injection, and
for twenty minutes afterward.''

"Someone made a death tape.''

"More to the point, someone has a death tape. Can
you imagine what they would fetch on the black market?''

Hayes looked thoughtful, and Vallenti was convinced

that if it was someone in Special Projects who had made the tape, the man sitting across the table from him didn't know anything about it.

Finally, Hayes looked up. "What makes you so sure that someone in the corporation did this?"

"Who else would have the technology?"

"In theory, it could be done on the outside."

"But in practice, it'd be just about impossible."

Hayes slowly put down his martini glass. "We are going to have to look into this."

Vallenti sipped his Scotch. He could see that Hayes was thoroughly rattled. That was how he wanted him. "My people already are."

"We need to talk to security."

Vallenti shook his head. "We don't talk to anybody. Not until we know who we can trust."

Hayes sighed and nodded. "Will you call me?"

"As soon as I hear anything more."

Hayes absently picked up the check. "This is a potentially very bad business."

Vallenti nodded. "Don't I know it."

THE SUPERSTAR WAS FAR FROM HAPPY. He slumped petulantly in the deep leather armchair and dug the pointed toe of his handmade Spanish boot into the thick, white pile of the wall-to-wall carpet. The double glazing of the hotel's penthouse suite presented an uninterrupted panorama of the city. Above the brown air layer the sun was warm and bright, and the sky was a perfect blue. A needle-thin rocket liner floated in the clear part of the sky. It was almost at eye level from where the superstar sat. Its wheels were down, its wings were out, and it was drifting in for a landing at Metro-4 airport, the one that handled the big sub-orbitals.

The superstar wasn't interested in the view, the sky, or the passing planes. He was being hassled by his manager in a one-on-one conference. He had already told his manager no way, four times. His manager wasn't inclined, though, to take no way for an answer.

"Listen, no way, Tom. I'm not going to do it."

"That's fucking dumb."

"Dumb or not, I don't like it."

"You're turning down ten million."

"It doesn't feel right."

"Don't you feel you're being a tiny bit irrational?"

"Sure I'm irrational. I'm a genius. If I was an accountant, I'd be logical, but I'm not and I ain't. Okay?"

"Jesus Christ, do you seriously expect me to go back to Combined Media and tell them that the deal's off?"

"You can tell them what you like. That's your problem."

The superstar hooked his leg over the arm of the chair and swiveled around so he was facing away from the manager. He stared out across the city. The rocket plane had gone, but otherwise it was exactly the same. While the superstar sulked, the manager marshaled himself for another attempt at persuasion. He loosened the collar of his fashionably casual lounging suit and ran his fingers through his long gray hair.

"Shall we try again?"

The superstar continued to pout. He was dressed in what amounted to a costly, spangled parody of the uniform worn by the gang kids from the welfare sections. They were, after all, the main solvent honking nucleus of his fans—the ones who consumed his tension tapes and fought their way into his live shows.

The manager's voice was comfortingly soft, more like

that of an analyst than a businessman. "You want to discuss it?"

Still the superstar refused to acknowledge him. The manager's voice hardened. "Can you hear me?"

"No."

"You don't want to discuss it?"

"I can't hear you."

"Aren't we being a bit childish?"

The superstar jabbed a heavily ringed finger at the manager. "You might be being childish. I'm not."

"What I'm primarily trying to do is to make you very rich."

The superstar didn't say anything, although this time he didn't look away. The manager pressed home his slight advantage.

"You want to be very rich, don't you?"

"I am very rich."

"You could be a lot richer."

"Not this way."

"How long is it going to take to convince you?"

"It's going to fucking take forever. My mind's made up. I won't do it."

"Have I ever pushed you into a wrong direction?"

"Sure you have. What about the Multisong deal? What about that terrible fuckup in Tokyo? You want me to go on?"

"That's hardly fair."

"You railroaded me into both of them."

Even the manager's seemingly boundless patience was starting to fray. "Will you do something for me, as a favor?"

"What?"

"Could you just take the time to explain in a little detail what exactly you have against this offer? It is, after all, the biggest thing you've ever been offered. From where I sit, it looks like the dream of a lifetime."

"From where I sit, it looks like a nightmare."

"Why, for Christ's sake?"

"I don't like the whole idea."

"You'll be the first living entertainer ever to be recorded on a feelie program. People will actually be able to feel what it's like to be you while you're performing. I would have thought your ego would have jumped at the chance."

"Don't knock my ego. It pays for your plastic surgery."

"You're still avoiding the question."

The superstar's rings flashed as he again stabbed an angry index finger toward his manager. "Who the hell do you think you are? Where do you get off cross-examining me like this?"

The manager also began to lose his temper. "I'm your fucking manager who's just set up a deal worth ten million plus and is sitting here while his client throws it back in his face without even offering a half logical explanation. Will that do?"

The superstar sneered. "Worried about your piece of the ten mil?"

"If you like, sure. I don't handle your affairs because I like it."

"You could always quit."

"I might as well do that if you keep on turning down money the way you are at the moment."

For the first time the superstar looked worried. His expression became placating. "Okay, okay, it doesn't have to go this far. There's no need for us to fall out."

"So, do I get an answer? I have to tell Combined Media something."

The superstar looked uncomfortable. He ran his fingers through his cropped hair. "Hell, I don't know. I can't put it into words. I ain't sure that I want people to know how I feel when I'm doing a show. It could destroy the mystery. Jesus, Tom, for all I know it could finish me. I don't think it's worth the risk."

"There's millions in it."

"It's too much like selling a piece of my soul."

"That's what primitive tribes used to think about being photographed."

"Maybe they were right."

"I've never noticed you avoiding being photographed."

"A feelie's something different."

The manager stood up and walked over to the window. Another rocket was coming in to Metro-4. At the other side of the sky a regular jet was on approach to LAX.

"You know what you're paying for your superstition?"

The superstar fiddled with one of his earrings. He tried to be placating. "Listen, forget superstition and all that stuff. Let's look at it another way."

The manager turned away from the window. "Okay." He went back to his chair, sat down, and looked receptive. "So tell me."

The superstar sat up straight in his chair. He avoided looking directly at the manager.

"We've always agreed that when I'm doing a live show, nothing should get in the way. It's me and the audience and nothing that'll sidetrack it, right?"

"That's right. I've always kept TV crews in check, turned down advertising tie-ins. It's been done exactly as you wanted it."

The superstar smiled triumphantly. "Okay then. How the hell can I do a live show if I'm hooked up to a bank of feelie recorders? If that ain't getting between me and the audience, I don't know what is."

"They have given me assurances . . ."

"Assurances? Tom, will you tell me what the hell assurances is supposed to mean?"

"The recording and monitoring equipment wouldn't impede your doing the show."

The superstar looked sideways at the manager. "You want to know something, Tom?"

"What?"

"I don't trust you when you use long words. I get the idea you're trying to con a poor boy from the welfare sections."

"You've come a long way from there."

"Don't bullshit me. What kind of setup is Combined Media offering?"

"I thought you weren't interested."

"Just tell me, will you?"

The manager was back on the defensive. "Okay, okay. You may not believe it, but I spent a solid three days making sure this deal would be acceptable. They tell me that all the hardware they need could be built into your stage suit. It would be miniaturized and, where necessary, disguised as zips, studs, jewelry and what have you. Also any bits you don't want made available will be erased. You have full control of the finished product."

"I'd still be trailing wires all over the stage. How the hell am I supposed to work like that?"

"There won't be any wires. It'll be a radio link between you and the recording banks."

"I thought that they had to stick things into your skull."

"There'd be one micro implant in the back of your neck. Fitting it is quite painless and could be disguised by a necklace or a high-collared shirt."

The superstar smiled wryly. "You've taken care of just about everything, haven't you?"

The manager shrugged. "That's what I'm paid for."

"I suppose you're going to ask me to reconsider now?"

The manager looked intently at the superstar. "There is one thing I ought to tell you."

The superstar raised an eyebrow. "What?"

"If you were to blow this off, Combined Media could get very mean about it."

"So?"

"They have a lot of influence among the networks."

"They couldn't hurt me."

"You're not that big."

"This is blackmail."

"They're like that."

The superstar swung his chair around and stared out of the window again. This time it wasn't a petulant gesture. He looked thoughtful. Finally he swiveled back to look at his manager.

"Listen, Tom, I got to think about this. I'll call you tomorrow."

WANDA-JEAN'S EYES WERE GLUED TO the monitor screen that was built into the game booth. The dazzling smile of Bobby Priest was filling the screen.

"Okay, we're back and it's time for Personality Fall Down."

The face of Priest dissolved into dozens of tiny repeating images. "Wildest Dreams" was heavily graphicized. It never let the viewer alone for a single moment, teasing, titillating, never really allowing the picture to come to rest, bouncing its audience around in a continual state of contrived excitement.

"Just to remind everyone how this part of the show works. You'll see four contestants in the booths in front of us."

Cut to the four contestants standing in transparent cylindrical pods. They were bathed in the beams of a dozen or more revolving searchlights, and CO_2 fog, sliced by slashing blue and gold lasers, drifted around them.

"I will start to read the personality profile of either a

figure from history or a current celebrity. Contestants can jump in at any time when they think they know the identity of the personality being profiled.''

Bobby Priest was filling the screen again. His teeth flashed like a neon sign and the sequins of his body tux dazzlingly reflected the lights and the lasers. He glowed like Mr. Electric.

''Sounds easy, right? Well, home folks, it would be easy if the contestants weren't standing over *the vat*!''

Bass electronics surged in a deep bowels-of-hell version of a Bach fugue. The close-up of Priest became a neon leer.

''The longer the contestant delays answering, the wider the floor on which they're standing slides open. Too long a delay or a wrong answer, and the floor vanishes altogether and the contestant goes down into *the vat*!''

The mists parted and the vat was revealed. It was a circular chromium-plated tank maybe five feet deep and twenty feet across. It was filled with a heavy viscous goop, about the consistency of molasses, primarily Day-Glo pink but streaked with lazy swirls of poisonous yellow and green that made it look like something from a toxic-horror show.

Bobby Priest dominated the screen again.

''Okay, contestants, are you ready for the next personality profile?''

Back to the four contestants. In unison, they all nodded brightly. The bass electronics picked up tempo, an urgent, anxious, rock 'n' roll pulse.

Bobby Priest's eyes had a twinkle that was scarcely pleasant.

''Don't forget, scenes from the life of each contestant are available on the current IE catalog.''

The contestants nodded again, less brightly this time.

''Okay, players. Here we go.''

On the waist-high panels in front of the contestants, four red lights came on. The audience noise that was pumped into the booths faded out. Each of them was alone in soundproof silence. Their four tense faces came on the monitor in a four-way split screen.

The voice of Bobby Priest came through loud and relentlessly clear.

"He was born in Clay County, Missouri, in 1847."

The floor under Wanda-Jean's feet split down the middle. Slowly but surely the gap started to grow wider.

"He married Zerelda Mimms in 1874."

The gap was now an inch wide, and Wanda-Jean could see right down into the vat. Bubbles slowly burst, leaving brief liquid craters. It looked like the surface of Jupiter in miniature, just six feet below her.

"During the war between the states he served with Bloody Bill Anderson in—"

There was a loud raucous buzzing. A green light came on beside a red one. Someone had hit the answer button. Wanda-Jean's head flashed around. The anxious face of the blond guy next to her came up on the screen. It was immediately replaced by the beaming Bobby Priest.

"Okay, okay. Paul here thinks he knows the answer. That's Paul Lindstrom, from right here in town. Shall we see if Paul's got the right answer, folks?"

The yell of the crowd agreeing with Priest crashed into Wanda-Jean's booth.

"Okay, Paul, what's your answer?"

"My answer's Jesse James, Bobby."

Paul's tense face came back onto the screen, then gave way to Bobby, leeringly building up the tension.

"Well, Paul . . ." He consulted a blue card in his hand. ". . . the correct answer is . . . Jesse James."

The applause was like a physical buffeting to Wanda-Jean, a punishing slap in the face for not having got the answer. The gap between her feet seemed to beckon oily, eager to claim her. There was a brief shot of the floor under Paul snapping shut, then Bobby Priest was back dominating the screen.

"Okay, contestants, here we go again, and let's see who'll be the first to fall down!"

The mob bayed its eagerness to see someone fall into the mud.

"Are you ready with the answer buttons?"

The contestants nodded again. Nobody could miss the answer button. It was right in the center of the flat shelf-like panel that ran across the front of each contestant's booth. On one side of the button were the lights that indicated that the question had been asked or answered and the speaker that relayed all outside sounds. On the other side was a seven-inch color monitor that showed the contestants what was being broadcast to the hundred million viewers.

Wanda-Jean caught sight of a medium shot of herself enclosed in the pod: long legs, blond hair, and white bodysuit. She looked like a thing in a test tube, something that had been created there, a vat-grown bimbo poised to be tipped back into the primal ooze that had spawned her.

"Okay then, let's go to question number two."

The sound of Bobby Priest's voice booming out of the pod's speaker jerked Wanda-Jean back to the reality of the moment. She had to concentrate. If she didn't answer one of the next four questions, she would drop through the wide open floor straight into the pink goop. If she answered wrongly, the floor would snap wide open straightaway. The only way was to get an answer right. A correct answer made the floor slide all the way shut again.

Question two seemed to confirm all Wanda-Jean's doubts. Paul hit the answer button right away and came up correct. The only consolation was that he came in fairly quickly. One didn't gain all that much headway over the competition if one answered fast. On the other hand, delaying could mean that another player would have the chance to jump in first.

There were five inches of space between Wanda-Jean's legs when Priest started into question three. It was just creeping up to six when Paul tried to score again. With a look of confidence, he gave out his answer. Confidence turned to horror as Bobby Priest gloatingly informed him that it was incorrect. The floor opened all the way. He hit the goop with a loud slap that was picked up by a dozen or more directional microphones around the rim of the tank and probably more submerged in the goop; the sound was amplified and enhanced and fed out over the air like a clap of doom. The audience jumped up in the bleachers, howling and waving fists and making the weird, high-pitched keening that was unique to the audience on ''Wildest Dreams'' as Paul dragged himself laboriously to the edge of the tank with his bodysuit disintegrating and his body plastered with the garish goop.

With Paul gone it left Nancy and the long-haired farm boy. Wanda-Jean told herself that she was just lucky. It had to end soon. Question four began. Nobody seemed anxious to hit the button. The gap in the floor got bigger and bigger. Wanda-Jean didn't have a clue to the answer. The gap was twelve inches wide before the farm boy made a stab for the button. He didn't wait for Bobby Priest's ritual. His voice was high-pitched and trembling.

''Abraham Lincoln.''

Bobby Priest didn't like any hick contestant getting in the way of his building up the suspense. For a fleeting instant his eyes narrowed, then his bland, all-encompassing smile spread across his face. He didn't actually jerk his thumb down like a Roman emperor. He didn't need to. It was there in his smile.

''I'm sorry, Billy . . .''

So that was his name.

''. . . It was Rameses II.''

Billy hit the goop and the crowd went wild. Bobby Priest seemed to swamp the screen.

"Well! Well! Well! They're sure going down like flies tonight. I guess it's a real fast one. But don't worry. If this game ends before time, we got more fun for you. Meanwhile stay tuned to see the ladies battle it out, after these messages."

There was a pause for the commercials. Wanda-Jean sagged against the back of the booth. It was impossible to relax when the floor of the booth consisted of two six-inch shelves on either side.

Wanda-Jean saw that Nancy was looking at her. Their eyes met. Wanda-Jean looked quickly away. There was no way that they could communicate. It was one or the other of them who would fall.

The floor manager's voice came over the speaker. "Fifteen seconds to air time."

Wanda-Jean straightened up and dragged her face back into the pleasant, eager expression. She avoided even looking at Nancy while Bobby Priest was welcoming back the viewers. The picture cut to a long shot of Wanda-Jean and Nancy standing like specimens in their glass cases. There was something almost sinister about the two empty booths. It reminded Wanda-Jean of some form of execution.

Bobby Priest was off again. "Just Wanda-Jean and Nancy—will one of them make it to the Dreamroad? Maybe question five will tell all.

"Okay, ladies. Are you ready for question five?"

They both nodded. Wanda-Jean saw she was in close-up and forced herself to smile. The smile faded abruptly when she saw the next shot. It was one of the tricky angle shots that were the hallmark of "Wildest Dreams." The cameramen claimed it was what really made the show so big, but who listened to the cameramen?

This particular one was shooting up through the gap of the booth floor and straight between Wanda-Jean's legs. It missed being hard-core by just a fraction. Not that "Wildest Dreams" minded being hard-core, but there were still enough old folks in the ratings for the producers to try and make it look accidental rather than played for, as they did on the youth shows.

Wanda-Jean wanted to look down, but she restrained herself.

"Okay, here's question five."

The red light went on. Wanda-Jean tensed. The floor started to move again.

"He spent the majority of his life in prison.

"His first sentence was at the Indiana Boys' Reformatory at Plainville in 1951."

The remaining ledges of the floor at either side of the booth were becoming alarmingly narrow.

"In 1960 he was convicted of forging government checks and jailed for ten years."

Wanda-Jean didn't have a clue. She did her best to resign herself to dropping into the mud and out of the show.

"Released in 1967 he started a hippie-style commune at Spahn Ranch, near Los Angeles."

Spahn Ranch tugged tentatively at a cord in her memory. Then, in a flash, it fell into place. She had seen a show—it couldn't have been more than a month earlier. Wanda-Jean couldn't believe her luck. She hit the answer button. The floor stopped moving. The remaining strips of floor were now so small that Wanda-Jean had to brace herself with one hand to avoid falling. She caught sight of her worried face in full close-up on the monitor. She quickly changed her expression. She was supposed to be enjoying the experience.

Bobby Priest joined her in split screen on the monitor.

"Well, in the nick of time, Wanda-Jean thinks she's got an answer. Shall we see if she's got it right or if she's going to *the vat*?"

The crowd howled enthusiastically.

"Okay then, Wanda-Jean. What's your answer?"

Wanda-Jean's arm was starting to ache. It wasn't easy,

staying on her precarious perch. "I think the answer's
Charles Manson, Bobby."

"She thinks it's Charlie Manson."

The audience howled mindlessly. Bobby Priest as-
sumed a sorrowful pose.

"Well, Wanda-Jean, I've got to tell you that . . ."

Wanda-Jean panicked. She felt sick. Then Bobby
Priest's face lit up.

". . . You're absolutely right!"

The crowd went wild right on cue. The floor under
Wanda-Jean slid back into place. She was able to move
around again. A shot of Nancy came up on the monitor.
She was in a bad way. She had both arms pressed hard
against the sides of the booth to keep her balance. The
moment the floor started to move again she would fall.
She probably wouldn't be able to reach for the answer
button without slipping. It was all over for Nancy. Wanda-
Jean allowed herself a quick triumphant grin. Almost as
soon as her expression shifted she found her smirking
image flashed up on the screen. There must have been a
cameraman waiting for her reaction. Wanda-Jean tried to
look like a good sport, but only succeeded in looking
shifty. Then Bobby Priest took over.

"Okay, here we go with the next question. Are you
ladies set to go?"

Wanda-Jean nodded, projecting keenness with all her
might. Nancy didn't bother to respond. She just clung
on with grim hopelessness.

"Okay, let's roll."

The red light came on. The floor started to move again.
The picture held firm on Nancy.

"She was born in . . ."

Nancy slipped. She grabbed for a handhold that wasn't
there. A spray of goop arched into the air as she hit the
tank.

Wanda-Jean hugged herself with delight. She was
caught in a blaze of lights. The booth was slowly lowered

until it rested on the rim of the tank of mud. Bobby Priest, with due ceremony, and carrying a small hand mike, came across the floor to help her out. He was followed by his own blaze of glory.

He stretched out a hand. Their glories merged. He turned to the camera.

"And it's Wanda-Jean who makes it to the Dream-road!"

Emoting with everything that she had, Wanda-Jean grabbed Bobby Priest and kissed him. "I can't believe it! I just can't believe it."

Priest fended her off with a practiced jesture that looked affectionate but actually stopped her from taking over the two shot. The credits started to roll, and the crowd howl swamped everything. Wanda-Jean suddenly looked puzzled. There seemed to be an undertow of boos beneath the general zoo hooting. What had she done? Bobby Priest lowered his mike and whispered in her ear without the slightest slip in his perfect professional smile.

"Don't worry about those morons, honey. You won, didn't you?"

Her confusion was suddenly compounded by a strong, if unfocused, sense of foreboding.

 "I'M HARDLY GETTING ANYTHING, Connie. Perhaps you ought to try a little harder."

Connie Starr raised her head. "For your information, I've been coming so hard I'm starting to feel dizzy."

"Not so I've been able to notice."

"Don't make me the scapegoat for your inadequacies."

"What's that supposed to mean?"

"It must be hard to be a dyke and frigid at the same time."

"You're quite replaceable, Connie."

"So replace me. Just try it."

"Tantrums aren't going to help."

"Perhaps a director who isn't dead from the neck down might."

"Shall we just calm down and try it again?"

Connie sighed and let her head fall back onto the pillow. She was lying on her back on a large translucent block of soft plastic that supported her weight but had sufficient elasticity to allow a high-quality electrostatic induction with the areas of her body that came in contact with it. It looked like a bed from some particularly perverse theme room in a love motel, or maybe a highly specialized gynecological operating table. In the business, the thing was known as the altar, which was a little more manageable than its official title, the Krupp Full Body Sense Receptor. Naked, Connie lay with her legs spread and one knee slightly raised. A mosaic of contact nerve pickups covered the upper half of her prone body, but they had been arranged in a way that gave her room for a good deal of movement. As Connie always said, "You can't keep still when you're coming." Two lightweight recording snakes ran to the permanently implanted receptors behind her ears. Nestled between her spread legs was a heavily customized Panasonic XC 400, the one with the multiform mushroom cushion head.

In the control room, behind the airtight double glazing, the technical crew watched the exchange in silence, avoiding looking directly at either of the two women. They ran checks and fine-tuned the settings on the big board; anything to avoid being embroiled in the confrontation. The crew had known from the outset that the match between performer Connie Starr and director Felicity Springer was a bad one. Felicity Springer simply wasn't good at orgasms. Action sequences, sure. Drugs and hallucinations were a piece of cake to Felicity. But either because of some built-in lack of sensitivity or an inability to truly connect, she had serious problems with getting down a memorable orgasm.

Felicity Springer sat in the rear of the control room in what was known as the director's throne. The throne was directly connected to the altar. In theory, everything that Connie felt, Felicity should have felt, too. Feeder lines ran to implants in her neck and also to suction contacts at her wrists and fitted in a band around her head. She was slim and boyish with rather masculine features and close-cropped blond hair. Corporation gossip had her running with a procession of pretty if airheaded starlets, none of whom seemed to last for more than a couple of weeks. Her girlfriends may have come and gone at an alarming rate, but where her work was concerned she was a painstaking perfectionist. Even her enemies admitted that she did appear to have infinite patience.

"Shall we go for another?" she suggested.

Connie, on the other hand, had no patience at all and was far from through bitching. "Do you realize that I've laid down the orgasms for ninety-three programs? Ninety-three fucking programs and no one else has ever complained."

Connie had been discovered during the early days of feelie experiments. She had been an unsuccessful stripper who had been coerced by an eager young researcher to try to get an orgasm on tape. She had taken to it like a duck to water. To everyone's amazement she seemed able to produce awesome, shuddering reactions almost to order with a minimum of help and encouragement. As the feelies went commercial, she rapidly became the uncrowned queen of computerized sex.

"I'm the best. You can't sit there and tell me I'm not getting it on. I'm Connie fucking Starr. I always get it on. Ask anyone. That's why I get forty thousand per, plus residuals."

"That's why I haven't thrown you off the set and brought in a replacement. That's why I'm putting up with all your shit."

"You wait until I see Renfield. You'll find out what shit is."

"All I've got to do is play him the tape. So far you've come up with nothing. Nada, zilch."

"That's a lie."

"All you have to do is play back the tape. You'll feel it for yourself. We're supposed to be doing Catherine the Great. The stuff you've been giving me could be dubbed into Rebecca of Sunnybrook Farm."

Ahmed, the chief engineer on this session of orgasm inserts, made the mistake of trying to act as mediator. "Maybe this just isn't happening. Perhaps the basic chemistry isn't there. We could just use an orgasm out of stock. I doubt anyone would notice if we juiced the sample enough."

He immediately became the object of both women's scorn.

Connie's face twisted into a sneer. "There's nothing wrong with my chemistry."

Felicity shook her head. "I don't use stock material."

Connie reached for the remote to the XC 400. "What the hell, let's give it one more try. This time I'll take this thing off stun."

Felicity was immediately encouraging. "All we need is one good solid teeth rattler and we're out of here."

The control room was filled with the soft hum of the vibrator as it was picked up by the talkback mike. It went on for a full ten minutes before Felicity angrily shook her head.

"It just isn't happening."

Out on the altar, Connie cursed loudly. "Maybe it's a goddamned technical fault."

In the control room Ahmed shook his head. "Everything registers on line, Connie. In fact, I'm getting good levels on everything you're doing. In fact, the only problem . . ."

He glanced back at Felicity, leaving the sentence hanging. Ahmed seemed to have decided that he was in a no-win situation. He probably wouldn't work with Felicity Springer again anyway, so he might as well keep in with Connie. Connie wielded a good deal of power around the corridors of IE.

Connie raised herself on one elbow. "Hey, Felicity, maybe you oughta go with the levels and just admit that you ain't getting close to it."

Felicity's face seemed stretched by keeping her anger under control. "Listen, eventually I'm going to have to mix this thing, and I can't mix what I can't feel."

Connie laughed. "You never said a truer word, dearie."

"Don't call me dearie, goddamn it."

Connie stretched lazily on the altar. "I'll tell you what I'll do, honey. I'll give it one more shot, and if that doesn't work, we're all going to have to do some radical rethinking." She turned her attention to Ahmed. "You better be paying attention, handsome, because I'm only going to do this once." She again picked up the remote on the XC 400. "This time I'm really going to take this sucker off stun, so be ready for the maximum. Okay?"

Ahmed nodded. "Okay."

Again the soft whine of the vibrator came over the talkback speakers. Connie's eyes closed; her hips began to rotate with a circular motion. The vibrator sound was augmented by small gasps of pleasure. Her raised knee was slowly swinging from side to side.

"This is . . . one hell of a way to . . . make . . . a

living. Hold on . . . I think . . . I think it's starting to happen. Yeah . . . I think . . . I'm . . . falling in love . . .''

Felicity didn't look impressed. "I don't . . . wait a minute.''

Her eyes closed and her fists clenched.

"Wait . . . a . . . *minute*!"

She began to rock from side to side on her stool. Her thighs involuntarily rubbed themselves together.

"Oh, Jesus—yes!"

"Oh!"

"Oh, yeah! Yeah!"

"Don't stop! Please!"

Connie and Felicity became a two-voice counterpoint of groans and whimpers. Then, simultaneously, both women's backs arched. They both cried out. Felicity's voice was low and deep in her throat; Connie's was a high-pitched wail. Finally they both slumped.

There was a long silence. Felicity sat with her head drooping on her chest. Connie was sprawled out on the bed. Finally Connie opened her eyes. She regarded Felicity from under heavy, languid lids.

"How did you like them apples, darling?"

"THEY OUGHT TO BE HERE BY NOW."

"There's a few minutes to go yet."

It was the very end of the shift. Ralph's speech was slurred. He made no attempt at even seeming sober. He sat propped up against a cabinet with his legs stretched out in front of him. Not only was he drunk, he was also querulous.

"If they don't turn up in the next couple of minutes, I'll just get up and fuck off."

"You shouldn't do that, Ralph."

"You just see if I don't."

"You know we ain't supposed to leave until the next shift comes on. It's against regulations."

Ralph sniffed. "So wait for them."

Sam blinked and looked unhappy. "I wouldn't like to stay here on my own."

Sam was in almost as bad a condition as Ralph. He too was slumped against a cabinet. His knees were drawn up so he was a fat, fetal ball. Ralph had occasionally noticed, when he was capable of noticing, that if he drank more, Sam swallowed more pills. When he was capable of wondering, which was less often than he was of noticing, even, he wondered if it was coincidence or cause and effect. Most of the time he didn't care anyway, particularly at the end of a shift. Each day seemed to drain off everything except hostility, hostility that he took out on Sam.

"There's always Artie. He's probably around somewhere to keep you company."

"I don't think I'd really like to be left alone with Artie."

"You might be, and sooner than you think."

"What's that supposed to mean, Ralph?"

"You'll find out."

"You ain't talking about quitting again, are you, Ralph?"

"Maybe."

"You won't quit, Ralph, you won't ever quit."

"Don't be so sure."

"You won't quit."

"What makes you so smart?"

"I just know."

"Yeah?"

Sam didn't answer. When Ralph looked up, he saw

Sam's eyes were shut. How could the bastard go to sleep a minute to leaving time? The silence between them was harder for Ralph to take than the conversation. He looked bitterly across the vault. He'd show them. He'd show all the bastards. Maybe he'd even quit tonight. He imagined himself strolling in the next day, suitably late, and telling the motherfuckers upstairs that he was through. He was so lost in his own fantasies that Sam startled him when he spoke.

"What about Artie, Ralph?"

"What about him?"

"We ought to do something about him. I ain't seen him in so long I even forget what he looks like."

Ralph scowled. "I remember what the perverted son of a bitch looks like."

"I wish he'd come back."

Before Ralph could answer he noticed something out of the corner of his eye. Across on the far side of the vault something was moving. A golf cart was silently making its way along the rows of cabinets.

"About time, too."

Sam raised his head. "Not Artie?"

"Of course not. Bob, Dave, and Ali finally decided to come to work."

The golf cart came closer. It was a bit more beat up than the immaculate white ones used by the clean-cut young men from upstairs, the ones who wore the starched white suits. Riding on it were three men. They were dressed in the same drab tan overalls as Sam and Ralph. They also had the same dead complexions that came from spending too much of their lives in an underground vault.

The golf cart finally rolled to a halt beside Sam and Ralph. The men climbed off the cart with the stiff weariness of those who have dragged themselves out of bed before they were good and ready. They all stared wanly at Sam and Ralph, who had not yet bothered to get to their feet.

"Jesus Christ, will you look at this sorry pair?"

"You fuckers can go home now."

"If you got homes."

Ralph got up with difficulty. He lurched a couple of unsteady paces and yawned. "You took your fucking time."

Ali, the biggest of the three and the one who normally took control, squinted at Ralph. "You drunk again, you sick bastard?"

Ralph stuck out his chin. "What if I am?"

"Just don't take it out on us. It ain't none of our business."

"Damn right it ain't."

Sam, by now, was also up on his feet. He looked around blinking.

"I guess it's time to go."

Ali glanced at Sam and then turned back to Ralph. "Don't he ever change?"

"Never."

Ali shrugged. 'I'll call in, then you guys can go."

"Just hurry it up, will you?"

Ralph's drunken aggression was starting to get on Ali's nerves. His lip curled into a sneer. "You had a heavy day or something?"

"Just cut the crap, and make the call."

Ali put his hand on the wall phone and then stopped. He turned and faced Ralph. "One of these days I'm going to lose patience with your bullshit and just blow the whistle on your drinking."

Ralph took a step back and made vague fending-off motions with his arms. "Lighten up, will you?"

Ali turned to Bob and Dave in outraged amazement. "Did you hear that guy? He's telling me to lighten up."

Bob shrugged. "What do you expect from a lush?"

Ralph advanced drunkenly on Bob with clenched fists. "Who are you calling a lush?"

Sam, moving with incredible speed for one with his

chemical balance, got between Ralph and the other three. He put a hand on Ralph's arm. "They don't mean nothing."

"Yeah?"

"Yeah."

Ralph turned and wandered away muttering to himself. Ali picked up the phone and waited. After a while someone at the other end appeared to answer. Ali straightened up.

"This is 5066. We're just changing shift."

There was a pause.

"5066! Why don't you listen?"

Another pause.

"We're changing over shift."

Pause.

"Right, Bob and Dave and Ali coming on and . . . That's right, this is me, Ali . . . Okay, and there's Sam and Ralph . . ."

Sam moved up beside Ali. "And Artie. Tell them 'Artie.' "

Ali's eyes rolled heavenward. ". . . and Artie are coming off. Okay?" He put his hand over the mouthpiece. "You still covering for that guy?"

"He's our buddy."

"Jesus Christ! What?" He took his hand away from the mouthpiece. "Say what? Yeah, sure, yeah. Sure everything's alright. Listen . . . No, you listen, just because you got trouble up there, don't take an attitude with me, boy. Okay! Okay!"

Ali banged the phone back into its cradle. Ralph looked interested for the first time in hours.

"Trouble?"

Ali raised an eyebrow. His eyebrows were particularly pronounced and bushy. They reminded Sam of a pair of furry caterpillars he had seen when he was a kid.

"You ain't heard?"

Ralph shook his head. "I ain't heard nothing."

"You had one die on you down here, didn't you?"

"Yeah, so what? It ain't no skin off my back. A stiff's got to die now and again. It stands to reason."

"The way I heard it, it ain't just now and again."

"Huh? We only had one die on us. What's all this about?"

"If you didn't drink so much, you might notice what's happening."

"Yeah, alright, you made your point. Just tell me what's going on."

Ali rubbed the back of his neck. Now that he had Ralph's attention, he was getting in a few licks of his own.

"You must have had these new spot check calls, right?"

"Right."

"But you never wondered why?"

"I thought they were just screwing us around."

"It goes further than that."

"It does?"

"That's what these guys over in 6120 told me. I see them in the cafeteria."

Sam interrupted. "We don't never go to the cafeteria."

Ali sighed. "Maybe you should. You might find out a few things." He turned back to Ralph. "Anyway, these guys—"

"The guys from 6120?"

"Right, these guys told me that there's a full-scale, power-assisted panic going on upstairs."

"So what's causing all this?"

"The stiffs keep snuffing."

"Dying?"

"Dying."

"You're putting me on."

"True as I stand here. 6120 had four croak in the last

month. By all accounts the same kind of thing's been happening in all the sections that got lifers.''

Sam tugged at his ear. ''Seems to me that lifers would be bound to die sooner or later. Nobody lives forever.''

Ralph grinned. ''He seems to be right for once. We all got to go sometime.''

Ali sniffed. ''It seems that upstairs is thinking that there's too many of them going sooner, and not enough of them later.''

''You figure there's something wrong in the system?''

''It sounds like it.''

For a brief instant Ralph had a vision of glory. He should do something about it. He could blow the whistle on all of it, the feelies, Combined Media, and the whole mess. He was confronted by an image of himself as the little man who brought down the giants, the fearless crusader who cut out the corporate rottenness and held it up for everyone to see. Then the bubble burst. If the corporation had a major problem, there'd be a major cosmetic job before anyone like him could do anything. So some stiffs died. Who would really give a damn, even if they got to hear about it at all?

For the duration of the heroic flash, Ralph had been standing straight and tall. As it faded, his shoulders slumped and he no longer cast a long shadow. He yawned and looked at Ali. ''Yeah, well, that's really fascinating, but we're having this conversation on my time. I got to go.''

Ali shrugged. ''If you don't want to know what's going on, it's your funeral.''

Ralph surveyed the rows upon rows of cabinets, each with its corpselike occupant. He grunted. ''Yeah, funeral. I'll be seeing you.''

''See you, Ralph.''

Sam had already climbed aboard the golf cart and was sitting behind the wheel. Sam seemed to be avoiding looking directly at him.

"I think I better drive, Ralph."

"Do what the fuck you like."

Ralph slumped into the seat beside Sam.

⬡ "SO THE NUMBERS WOULD SEEM TO confirm what we've already been thinking about Wanda-Jean?"

"Couldn't be closer."

"So we start the program?"

"Absolutely. Build her for the fall."

There were four of them at the meeting. Dan Henderson, the producer of "Wildest Dreams"; Shala Groton, the contestant supervisor; and Paul Nitz, the chief contestant handler. Murray Dorfman served as gofer. The meeting was taking place in Henderson's cluttered office. The desk was littered with used napkins, coffee cups, and plastic containers. They had ordered in an early lunch from the Cuban restaurant down on Ford Street.

Henderson thought for a moment. "How many shows do you think we can run with this bad girl thing before it gets tired?"

Nitz shrugged. "That depends on the tabloids. If Bones Bolt gets his hooks into her, it could run and run. At the most modest estimate, I think we could let her go for four. People are really starting to dislike her."

Henderson nodded. "What are the samplings on this? I mean, let's get real, guys. Dislike don't signify diddley if it can't be built into real hate. What's the base beef?"

Dorfman cleared his throat. "According to last night's nationwides, she is thought of as an opportunist and untrustworthy. They also think that she has designs on

Bobby himself, although everyone knows that Bobby's too smart to fall for a cheap slut like her. The analysis indicates that a good deal of the resistance is rooted in a simple visual quirk. There is something about the configuration of her eyes and nose that makes her look shifty on TV.''

Henderson smiled sadly. ''Ain't the viewing public wonderful?'' He glanced at Nitz. ''You think she can stand up to what we have in mind?''

Paul Nitz picked up a slice of fried plantain. ''She's tough. I figure she'll go through anything to stay on the show. She's got a very bad self-image, however. The process could turn her into a basket case when it's all over.''

Dorfman quickly nodded. His smirk was oily. ''I can vouch for her bad self-image.''

Henderson looked at him coldly. ''I'm sure you can, Murray. I'm sure you can.''

Henderson disliked Murray Dorfman. The fawning little weasel really deserved to be fired. Henderson had thought of firing Dorfman before, but somehow there always seemed to be something more important to do at any given time. He sipped his coffee. It was getting cold. He wanted this meeting over with.

''You don't think that she'll actually crack on the show? We can't have that. It makes us look like the bad guys.''

Groton shook her head. ''I really doubt it. She's kind of dogged. I was wondering if it might be an idea to let her in on the game.''

Henderson shook his head. ''No way. I really can't go with contestant collusion unless it's unavoidable. As far as Wanda-Jean is concerned, she's playing a straight-arrow game. Keep her wondering why the folks just don't seem to like her.''

Nitz started gathering up the debris of his lunch. ''Four shows and then review the situation?''

Henderson nodded. ''It's a good start.'' He didn't even bother to look at Dorfman. ''Murray, get on to PR and tell them to start leaking Bad Bad Wanda-Jean stories to the media, see if they'll bite.''

Dorfman nodded eagerly. "Right away, Mr. Henderson.''

"That's right, Murray. Right away.''

MALLORY SLICED THE GRAPEFRUIT IN half. It was done with a frightening precision. Dustin sipped his coffee and wondered if she had been a surgeon in another life, or maybe an executioner. She placed the two halves side by side on the black Finwear plate and regarded them with a pursed-lipped expression of displeasure.

"I swear these things get smaller and smaller.''

She reached for the box of Kellogg's Hi-Bran. Dustin thought that nothing would please Mallory on this particular morning. Three days had passed, and he was still being punished for his inattention following the Fedder's dinner party. How many days was he supposed to spend in hell for that transgression? On top of that, she had once again taken up the Cosmopolitan Deprivation Diet, and he was expected to starve right along with her. He repressed an urge to pick up one of the grapefruit halves and squash it into her face. Instead, he sipped his coffee and looked docile.

"It's probably the result of a marketing decision taken after months of consumer research,'' he offered.

"If I wanted a small, sour, yellow orange, I'd ask for one. I want my grapefruit the way they always were.''

Mallory picked up the *Times* and turned to the op-ed page. She folded the newspaper with the same precision with which she had sliced the grapefruit. She read for a couple of minutes and then spoke without looking up.

"Here's something for you, Dustin. Wintek has done a piece on the feelies. He seems to think that we all ought to reconsider our positions and that maybe they aren't so bad after all."

Dustin sighed. "Wintek is a liberal asshole."

He knew that Mallory had no interest whatsoever in the thoughts of Herman Wintek and didn't give a damn about the feelies. All that was happening was that he was being set up for another round of her insidious sarcasm. Mallory looked at him over the top of her rimless glasses, the kind that George Bush used to wear. The style had made something of a comeback over the last summer.

"I guess he doesn't have the intellectual scope of a thinker like Bones Bolt."

"Mallory, I—"

"Dustin, please don't make hangdog faces at me. I only mentioned Wintek's column because I thought it might appeal to your new-found obsession with the feelies."

"I don't have an obsession with the feelies."

"Don't pout at me, either."

"I'm not pouting, and I don't have an obsession with the feelies."

"You did the other night. You were certainly more interested in some dumb TV show about them than you were in me."

"How many times do I have to tell you that I was just tired and a little drunk?"

"You weren't too tired to be trying to cop a peer down the front of Laramie Fedder's dress all through dinner. What was it? Are you and Martin trying to organize a little matrimonial swapmeet? If you are, you can forget it. I have no interest in sleeping with Martin Fedder even to titillate you. God knows I do enough to go along with your little perversions, but there are limits."

This was an entirely new charge and also a complete fabrication. What in hell would he be doing looking down the front of Laramie Fedder's dress, for Christ's sake? Mallory was a hundred times better-looking. That was part of the trouble. She even looked good right now, with her loose, sleep-tousled, honey blond hair and practically transparent black lace peignoir offset by the aloof expression and the George Bush reading glasses. A part of him would have liked to have reared across the breakfast nook and had her right then and there among the Finwear dishes, the Gunden place settings, the too-small grapefruit, and the Hi-Bran, but there was no chance of that. She probably wouldn't let him near her for at least a week, and even then it would only be after a considerable period of begging. A lesser woman might have given in to her own needs long before the week was up, but not Mallory. She wasn't the kind to let mere lust come between her and total moral victory. Mallory had once confided in him during the aftermath of passion that when she was a little girl, her ambition had been to be Margaret Thatcher when she grew up. And what did she mean she went along with his little perversions? She had more than a few little quirks of her own.

"Mallory, this is starting to get ridiculous."

She ignored him, slowly lowering the paper and taking off her glasses. "I heard from Daphne Ziekle that Christopher Elwin, the idiot who's been running Elwin Systems into the ground since his father died, finally turned his holdings over to the control of his brother and took a life feelie contract."

"I keep telling you that I'm not interested in the feelies." In fact, Dustin was very interested in the feelies at that moment—anything that would spare him psychwar over breakfast. A life contact seemed very appealing. Maybe he should be Caligula or some Turkish sultan with a very large harem.

Once again, Mallory ignored him. She looked

thoughtful. "Maybe Wintek's right. Of course, not for the reasons that he's putting forward. They're twentieth-century bleeding heart nonsense. It could be, however, that their real function is to take the inadequates out of circulation. It could be a way to return to the survival of the fittest without anyone actually getting hurt. When the news came out that Elwin had taken the contract the company's stock went up nine points. What I don't see is why they've made them so expensive. Sure, I can see the value in taking rich idiots off the streets, but why in hell don't they offer it to the underclass? Let the damned epsilons be rapists and junkies while safely locked up in a plastic coffin instead of roaming the streets unchecked and doing it for real."

"Maybe that's the eventual plan. Maybe CM is just creating a market pressure."

"Well, all I can say is that I wish they'd hurry up. It's not safe to go out, even around here."

Mallory's face actually contorted when she talked about the underclass as though the very thought of them put a bad taste in her mouth. Dustin realized that the woman he had married was a real Nazi at heart. He didn't know whether to feel proud or frightened.

 "THEY DON'T LIKE ME!"

"You've got a page and a half in *Game World*."

"They're calling me the bad girl of 'Wildest Dreams.' Mean Wanda-Jean. What did I ever do to them?"

Brigitte the chaperone/dresser/gofer sat down on the bed. "I've been with maybe a dozen contestants while they were on the Dreamroad. The fan rags always cook up some kind of personality for them. You don't want to let it get to you.''

Brigitte had been provided by the network. She came with the hotel suite and the bodyguard who waited outside the door. It was what you got when you started on the Dreamroad. Wanda-Jean found that she had been removed from her normal life and shut away in luxurious isolation. Her only contact with the outside was either through the show or through Brigitte.

Wanda-Jean threw the magazine on the floor and pouted. "I never heard of a bad girl winning in the end."

Brigitte looked genuinely scandalized. "Don't talk like that."

"Why not? It's true, isn't it?"

"Of course it's not. Anyone can win."

"It's just that it feels really unlucky to be the bad girl."

Brigitte stood up. "Maybe I should fix you a drink?"

"I shouldn't start drinking this early in the day."

"It's the middle of the afternoon."

"Yeah, but I only just got up."

It seemed to Wanda-Jean that just about everything in her life had been turned upside down. From being anonymous she now appeared on TV and had her picture in fan magazines. She seemed to sleep all day and live by night. Where once she had been on her own, making her own decisions and facing her own problems, now all she had to do was order from a menu, or come up with a yes or no answer when someone offered to mix her a drink, fetch her a pill, or run out for a magazine. The network didn't expect Wanda-Jean, or any of the other contestants, to think for themselves while they were on Dreamroad. The network's minions acted accordingly.

The real physical change was the hotel suite. The downtown Sanyo-Hyatt was a far cry from the minuscule singles apartment in the faceless high rise. The big openplan day room almost gave her agoraphobia. It seemed

as big as a football field. The wraparound, ceiling to
floor, double-glazed windows and the wall-to-wall, dark
green carpet added to the sense of space and exposure.
The fashionably sparse, ultra modern furniture didn't help
to give the place any sense of coziness.

Even the bedroom wasn't any refuge. It was as big as
her own apartment. The bed alone could accommodate
maybe five people in comfort. Just to make matters
worse, Brigitte felt she could walk in anytime she wanted
to. Wanda-Jean didn't have any place in which she could
feel confident she was alone. She had even offered to
trade the vast bedroom for the suite's much smaller second room, the one in which Brigitte slept. But Brigitte
had told her that it was impossible—she would be fired
if anyone found out. The inability to even organize a
simple thing like switching rooms made Wanda-Jean feel
even more like a prisoner of luxury. There was, of course,
also Brigitte herself, a short woman with pale skin, orange hair, and an air of continual confidence, a combination of nurse, nun, big sister, and warden.

Wanda-Jean lay on her side and watched Brigitte
moving around the room. Brigitte was a compulsive ti-
dier. She seemed incapable of just sitting still and
slouching. If nothing else was going on, Brigitte would
get up and tidy. It got on Wanda-Jean's nerves. A lot of
things about Brigitte got on Wanda-Jean's nerves. Sometimes she wondered if that was the way condemned prisoners felt. They used to be watched nonstop by obliging
guards. The thing Wanda-Jean couldn't get over was that
Brigitte had sat with a dozen other contestants before her.
She propped herself up on one elbow.

"How many of the contestants won?"

Brigitte looked around blankly. "What?"

"The contestants you've looked after—how many of
them won?"

Brigitte came over to her and briskly plumped up a
pillow. "Aren't you getting a little morbid, dear? All this

talk about being the bad girl, and bad luck, and now this. I'd think about something else if I were you. Why don't you watch TV or something? There's 'Penal Colony' on channel 80. You like that?''

Wanda-Jean stuck out her lower lip. "I don't want to watch TV. I want to know how many of the contestants who've been through your hands have won. Okay?''

"Isn't this all a bit childish?''

"How many won, goddamn it?''

As Wanda-Jean's voice got more hysterical, Brigitte's, in direct proportion, became more soothing.

"I can't tell you that.''

"Why not?''

"It's against the rules, dear.''

Wanda-Jean tried wheedling. "You can tell me, Brigitte. Nobody will find out.''

"I can't, and you know that.''

"Then fuck you, you miserable bitch. You probably put a jinx on all of them.''

"You ought to start to grow up, dear. Neither of us needs this sort of thing.''

Wanda-Jean rolled over so her back was toward Brigitte. She lay in sullen silence for a long time, until a new idea struck her.

"I want to go out.''

Brigitte's patient look switched on. "You know you can't do that.''

"So I'm a prisoner?''

"You're not a prisoner. You have to stay inside for your own protection.''

"Who's going to hurt me?''

"Fans, psychopaths, people who've bet on the show, you want a list?''

"How am I supposed to get any exercise if I can't get out?''

"You know damn well that there's a gym, a swimming

pool, and a sauna in the basement of the hotel. You can use them anytime.''

"I just can't stand being cooped up in here. It's driving me crazy.''

"If you don't like the rules there's a very obvious solution.''

Wanda-Jean raised a quizzical eyebrow. "What solution?''

Brigitte smiled. It was a calm, superior smile. "You can always quit the show. Go back to your job and your little apartment and forget the whole thing ever happened.''

Wanda-Jean glared at her. "You'd really like that, wouldn't you?''

"I don't care either way. It's not my job to get involved.''

"Yeah?''

"You can believe what you like.''

Wanda-Jean lay flat on her back and stared at the ceiling. Brigitte moved busily about the room. All Wanda-Jean could think about was how ridiculous the whole situation was. She was supposed to be a star, the fan magazines told her that, and yet she wasn't even allowed to enjoy it.

The bodyguard stuck his head around the door. The bodyguards were changed regularly, but they all had the same flat, faceless, unapproachable expression, close-cropped bullet head, and massive shoulders. They reminded Wanda-Jean of retired ball players.

"There's a visitor coming up.''

Wanda-Jean sat up. "Who is it?''

"It's a Mr. Priest.''

"I'm not sure I want to see him.''

Brigitte stepped in. "Send Mr. Priest right through.''

"Sure.''

Wanda-Jean jumped angrily to her feet. "Don't I get any say in the matter? I said I didn't want to see him.''

"You don't say that to Bobby Priest."

"Jesus . . ."

"Hi, there. Is everybody happy?"

Bobby Priest was already in the room. He was almost as flamboyant off set as he was on. His white lounging suit would have cost a month's salary for Wanda-Jean at her old job.

Wanda-Jean was still standing glowering at Brigitte with clenched fists. Brigitte managed a calm greeting.

"Good afternoon, Mr. Priest."

"Hi there, Brigitte. Do I detect some tension in the air?"

"I think Wanda-Jean is starting to feel the strain. The fan rags weren't very kind to her."

Bobby Priest was the picture of caring concern. He put a protective arm around Wanda-Jean. "You don't want to let those things get to you. They got to write something or they wouldn't stay in business."

Wanda-Jean crumpled. She sat down on the bed. "It's not just that. It's the whole thing, being shut up in here, not having any life of my own. It just gets so hard."

"You'll be the one who's laughing, when you win."

"If I win."

"You got to think positive."

"Everyone seems to want to tell me what I got to do."

Bobby Priest sat down beside her. He took hold of her hand and stroked it. "Just relax, babe. Take one thing at a time and you'll be okay."

"You don't know what it's like. It's the waiting, the not knowing what's going to happen to you."

"You think I don't have troubles?"

Wanda-Jean dropped her head into her hands. "Yeah, I suppose so. I've just got myself wound up."

Bobby Priest patted her shoulder and got up. "I think I know what you need. You need to get out of here for a while."

Wanda-Jean looked up sharply. "I've been saying that all day. I just get told that it's against the rules."

"Not if you're with me."

Wanda-Jean half smiled. She almost, but not quite, fluttered her eyelashes. "Are you asking me for a date, Mr. Priest?"

Bobby Priest hit a formal pose. "I'd be honored if you'd permit me to take you to dinner tonight, ma'am."

Wanda-Jean laughed. "I'd be honored to come."

Instantly Bobby Priest was back again being his high-speed self. "Good. I've got to move now. I'll pick you up at eight."

"I'll be ready."

"Yeah, right."

It seemed as though Wanda-Jean was dismissed already. With mixed feelings, she watched Priest hurry out of the suite.

RALPH EMERGED FROM THE RT EXpress station to the all-too-familiar crowding, the piled-up trash, and the relentless decay. Even the booze and the contempt that familiarity was supposed to breed didn't stop the dull fear that always nagged at his gut on the ride home. The fear started fairly soon after the monorail pulled out of Reagan Plaza. That was the last outpost of downtown civilization. After Reagan Plaza, the twilight sprawl started, the miles of urban wasteland, the seemingly endless expanse of burned-out shopping malls, twentieth-century high-rise towers that loomed like giant crumbling headstones, and the equally beat-up durafoam adobes that were the sad legacy of the

Cuomo Administration's final, doomed crusade for national urban renewal. From Reagan on, only the underclass rode the rail, and they had long since been told to go and lose themselves. The cops had been pulled off the trains and it was a safe bet that there was no one watching the security monitors. The farther out one went from Reagan Plaza station, the more the fear grew. The cars became increasingly empty, and the dwindling numbers of passengers became more and more vulnerable to attacks by gangs of railjammers, bloods, and locos. Once upon a time, robbery had been the motive. Now most of the passengers who went all the way out to Lincoln Avenue, 207th Street, Southend, or the Point had very little worth stealing. That didn't, however, stop the attacks. The weirdies were on the rail, and they were so unpredictable they could do just about anything to the lone riders that were unfortunate enough to be on a train they took it into their heads to wild through.

Down on street level, the rail curved away, over the roofs of buildings that sagged against each other, apparently kept up only by encrusted grime and a miracle. Lincoln Avenue had once been a prosperous neighborhood shopping strip, but it had become a picture of desolation. The few stores that were still open were protected by steel grilles on the outside and armed guards within. Layers of graffiti covered every flat surface. Winos and derelicts shuffled on the cracked sidewalks, and groups of young men stood on street corners in immobile surly groups. Their fury at simply being alive was only temporarily damped down by Serenax, Blind Tiger, and Night Train.

As his own booze haze wore off, it left behind a nagging depression, the kind of depression where every problem, big or small, becomes insurmountable. He brooded for a minute or so on how Sam didn't like him. He meant to be pleasant to Sam, but, always, it ended up with him picking on the guy. He had even left Sam standing on the street that night. He had walked off without saying so much as "Good night" or "See you later."

Ralph's depressions had a habit of jumping from subject to subject. From Sam he moved on to the stiffs who were dying. Ralph had been brought up on the old TV late shows, the fearless private eyes who stumbled across a telltale clue to corruption in high places, or the courageous reporters who brought down governments. They had always fought their way through against all the odds; they stripped away the façade and showed the world the rotten side of the big and powerful.

Ralph's train of self-pity was interrupted by a physical annoyance. For the second time that week, the moving walkway had broken down. It was typical. The only money that got spent in this city got spent on the rich. All the poor people got was cheap shit that broke down, if it ever worked at all. Ralph started the long trek down the tunnel to the boarding point.

As he walked, his mind grasshoppered from one cause of resentment to another. Sam, the job, he couldn't help it. It wasn't his fault that he wasn't Philip Marlowe or Mike Hammer, or Bernstein and Woodward. Sure it would be great to get at Combined Media. He would like to be a hero, to smash the structure and show everyone its corrupt, disgusting inside. It wasn't his fault he didn't have friends in the police department, or work on a fearless, fact-finding TV show. He was just a drunk in a dead end, union nonjob who was frightened of the ride home at night. Nobody could expect him to overturn the system.

He turned the corner and saw the CRAC squad down the block: City Riot And Combat. There must have been a baby riot or radical wilding for them to be out. The presence of a couple of fire trucks and the smell of smoke in the air seemed to confirm that. He started cautiously down the block. The CRAC squad members were spread out over the street. It was doubtful that those paramilitary supercops would let him through to take his usual route to his building. In places like Lincoln Avenue, the regular PD behaved like an occupying army. The CRAC squads were more like alien invaders, vicious and violent, who moved in and crushed disturbance with an iron fist and not even the public relations nicety of a velvet glove. CRAC men were built for business. Every one of them was well over six feet tall, anonymous, and threatening in dark blue coveralls, full-body flak jackets, and paler blue, bone-dome helmets with built-in radios. The majority carried over-and-under M20s that were capable of firing tear gas and concussion grenades, although a few had street sweepers, heavy, rapid-fire shotguns that were more than capable of doing exactly what their name implied. The CRAC team's faces were hidden behind gas masks, which not only added to their air of invaders from space but also protected them from recognition when the inevitable charges of police brutality were raised after one of their actions. Something bad had definitely gone down. Sal's Pizza was a burned-out ruin; Ralph could see four bodies lying on the street. A teenage girl huddled on the sidewalk would not stop screaming. An officer went over to her. He hit her once, a quick jab with the butt of his weapon, and she was immediately silent. Ralph didn't even speculate how the trouble had started. Such sudden flares of violence could come out of nowhere—a word or a gesture, and the next moment there would be slaughter. Automatic weapons were common in these areas; even the kids carried them.

"Hey, you! Get out of here!"

The voice was muffled by the gas mask, but Ralph had no doubt that the cop's gesture was aimed at him. He pointed down the street in a single attempt to maintain a shred of dignity. "I live right down there."

"I don't give a damn where you live. Get the hell off the street."

Ralph knew it was pointless to protest. As he turned, he remembered the Vietnam movie that he had seen a few days earlier on the late show when he had been up with insomnia. What was that phrase they had used? Winning the hearts and minds of the population?

◆◆◆ FRANCIS XAVIER BARSTOW WENT INTO A
◆◆◆ feelie once a year. It was the shortest one avail-
◆◆◆ able, just six hours. He had to save all year to be able to afford it. Of course, he'd have liked to have actually experienced it on Easter weekend, but that wasn't possible. There were extra charges for his particular feelie if you had it on Easter weekend.

Francis Xavier Barstow had been through the same feelie so many times that he almost knew it by heart. The yelling of the crowd, the smell of the primitive city, the chafing of the rough, homespun robe, the pain of the whip cuts across his back, and, above all, the weight of the huge, wooden cross that bowed his shoulders.

He knew that a lot of people thought he was crazy. His neighbors and the people he worked with all thought he was a religious fanatic. He found some consolation in telling himself that they would think that about anyone who still tried to worship a god. Religion played no big part in this soulless age.

Sometimes he worried about his annual adventure in the feelie. He knew he was supposed to live in the image of Christ. Sometimes he wasn't too sure that it was right to seek the help of a lot of electronic gadgetry.

He'd asked the priest, but the priest hadn't been much help. He was one of the new kinds of priest, all psychology and social conscience. He told Francis Xavier that there was no harm in the feelie, but Francis

Xavier had suspected that the priest didn't think there was much good in it either.

Francis Xavier knew in his heart that he was right. They had invented the feelies, and the least he could do was use them to get closer to his god. It was better than all those other people who wanted to be samurai killers, prostitutes, and perverted Roman emperors.

Sometimes he felt that he was bracketed with those people. He didn't like the way the receptionist women looked at him when he went in to book his feelie time. He got the impression that he was seen as some sort of sexual weirdo, a masochist or something.

This time there seemed to be something a little different about the experience. What was left of his conscious mind couldn't quite get a grip on what exactly had changed. Somehow everything was a trifle more intense. The colors were brighter and appeared to shimmer. The pain was much more severe than he remembered. In previous experiences, it had been a tolerable background. In this one, it was almost more than he could stand.

The part of his mind that was still Francis Xavier Barstow pretty much knew the sequence of the crucifixion program by heart. He was coming up to the part where he stubbed his toe and stumbled under the weight of the cross.

Just like every time before, he found himself staring down at his dirty sandaled feet. There were flecks of dried blood. The ground was dry and cracked. Each footstep produced small puffs of dust. Then a small green lizard scuttled from under a rock. As far as he could sluggishly remember, that had never happened before.

Francis Xavier wasn't about to ponder on the significance of these changed details. In the middle of a feelie, it wasn't possible to ponder on anything. The greater part of his consciousness was too busy being Jesus Christ on the home stretch to Calvary.

He could see the small rock coming up. There was
nothing he could do to avoid it. His foot hit it and . . .

Pain, flashing burning jagged colors swamped the desert landscape and the brown faces that pressed in on him.
A scream like ripping steel blotted out all other sounds.
There was nothing else but stabs of red, orange, and
yellow, rolling sweeps of purple split by white forked
lightning, and the unbearable pain.

Then it stopped, just as suddenly as it had started. He
also found that he was more than a dozen yards farther
up the road. It was like a sudden jump in a film. Something was wrong. A much greater part of him was now
detached from the Christ personality.

The things around him were also changed. The visual
images seemed washed out, insubstantial, almost transparent. The sound was fuzzy and muffled. There was
enough of Francis Xavier Barstow outside of the feelie
to know that something was wrong. There wasn't enough
of him to know what to do. He felt he ought to scream
or thrash about. There ought to be an alarm, a button he
could push or a lever he could pull. Instead he just kept
plodding toward the Place of the Skull, until the pain
started again.

If anything, it was worse than the first time. The colors
and the noise were even more violent. The detached part
of his mind wasn't detached enough not to suffer. It felt
as though a blowtorch was being run lovingly over every
nerve ending in his body. He was convinced he was about
to die.

Then it stopped again. The color and noise vanished
as though it had never existed. There had been another
jump. He was lying spread on the cross. Two Roman
soldiers knelt beside him. There was something reassuring about the burnished bronze, well-polished leather,
and coarse red fabric of the uniforms. Francis Xavier had
asked for their forgiveness so many times that they almost felt like friends. He even knew their faces. One had

a deep brown, earthy face with a broad flattened nose like an ex-boxer. The other's was thinner, more sensitive . . . But it wasn't. He wasn't the same. He had a ridiculous false mustache and eyebrows. A fat cigar was clenched between his teeth. The absurd eyebrows were jerked rapidly up and down. The face split into an insane grin.

"Would you mind crossing your feet? We've only got three nails!"

SAM LET HIMSELF INTO HIS MINUSCULE room. Max the black and white cat was lying curled up on the bed with his tail draped around the tip of his nose. He woke up, yawned, and then got to his feet stretching languidly. He padded toward Sam, flexing his claws and digging them into the covers. Sam sat down on the bed. The cat butted his upper arm. Sam smiled and patted him.

"Hi, Max, how you been?"

The cat yowled.

"Hungry, huh?"

The cat yowled again. Sam picked him up.

"You better keep the noise down, or we'll both be in trouble."

He tried to pet the cat, but Max squirmed out of his arms. Still yowling, he ran to the small alcove the landlord liked to call a kitchenette, and then back to Sam.

"Will you shut up, Max? When are you going to realize you're against the rules?"

Sam climbed reluctantly to his feet, still trying to hush the cat. Max danced around his feet, alternately yelling and purring loudly. Sam opened a small wall cupboard with a cracked glass door and took out a pack of Kitty Krunch. He filled a small plastic bowl. The bowl was red and bore the legend "Present from Rio de Janeiro." Sam couldn't remember where the bowl had come from. He had certainly never been to Rio. He set the bowl down in front of the cat. Max threw himself, single-mindedly, into the task of eating. It was the high point of his day.

Sam went back to the bed and sat down. He watched the cat. In between mouthfuls, it would pause to purr joyfully. Cats, in fact pets of all kinds, were totally outlawed from all cheap-lease rooms. The rules had been made some ten years before, when an urban rabies scare had started City Hall on a vast antipet drive. The campaign had not worked, but the rules remained. Max was Sam's single, but continuous, act of rebellion.

Sam worried about Max. The cat had been with Sam for almost three years. Nobody had said a word about Max, but still Sam worried. As well as his sole act of rebellion, the cat was also his main source of companionship. Sometimes Sam wondered how he would survive without Max.

When those thoughts started, he would take a Serenax. The room was drab and as clean as it was possible to make a cheap-lease, where the war against roaches alone was a full-time occupation. The yellowing walls didn't bother Sam. He found them kind of restful. It actually was not hard to keep the room neat. Sam didn't have very much. Aside from the bed, two chairs, a small table, a built-in wall TV, and a selection of cooking utensils, there was just a small nest of shelves that held the meager mementoes of a life of very limited expectations. There was a blue plastic lunch box from an ancient TV show called "The Galaxy Rangers" that Sam had watched as a child, a Michael Jackson funeral mug, a glow-in-the-dark figurine of Batman with one arm missing, a group of lead spacemen, a neat row of books, and a framed black-and-white photograph of May Marsh, the star of "Penal Colony." He really didn't know why he kept that picture. He didn't actually like "Penal Colony."

Sam wondered if he should fix himself a meal. Somehow he couldn't be bothered. He had taken too many pills already. He just didn't have the motivation. Instead, he went to the same cupboard that held the Kitty Krunch and took down a jar of cookies. The cat looked up at him. Max had a keen interest in anything to do with food. Sam looked at him sadly.

"I only saw her once today, the girl in the vault, the one I told you about."

He munched absently on a cookie, carrying the jar with him as he went back to the bed.

"I have to go and see her when Ralph's off drinking, otherwise he gives me a hard time."

The cat sat down and began to wash himself.

"It's difficult with Ralph. I mean, he's my partner, and I like him, but when he drinks, he can get real mean. I tell myself it ain't his fault, but it still ain't easy. I like to look at the girl."

The cat was totally involved in its toilet. Max always did a thorough job.

"I sure hope nothing happens to her."

Sam started on another cookie. As he chewed, he stared at the cat.

"You're just not interested, are you?"

Sam reached out and turned on the TV. One of the consolations of a cheap-lease was the way almost everything could be reached from the bed.

The screen came to life. It was channel 45, "Earth News." It was in the middle of an item about a subway riot. Sam was glad he didn't use the subway. It was worth the extra fare to take the monorail and know he was fairly safe. On the subway, anything could happen.

The picture on the screen seemed to be proving Sam's point. It was shaky and hand held. It showed a seven-man CRAC squad clubbing a subway car full of fighting passengers into some semblance of order. The commentary mentioned Lincoln Avenue station.

"I hope Ralph wasn't involved."

Sam flipped the channel. On 48 someone was getting his head kicked in an ancient western. Sam turned off the set. He didn't like violence.

He reached for the bookshelf. Sam was reading two books at the moment. One was *The House at Pooh Corner*, the other was *Moby Dick*. Sam didn't feel like dealing with Herman Melville, so he picked up *Pooh Corner*. He opened the book, took out a marker, and settled back to read. The cat climbed on his chest and rolled onto the open book. Sam smiled and poked the cat in the stomach.

"What's the matter, don't you want me to read?"

The cat waved its legs in the air and tried to bite him.

"Maybe you want to watch television?"

 WANDA-JEAN SAT UP IN THE HUGE BED. She felt a little dizzy. She had drunk too much, earlier in the evening. Over on the other side of the bed, Bobby Priest was fast asleep.

She looked over at him. In repose, he was very different from the character she had come to know on the studio floor. Without the surface layer of fast-talking energy, he looked weak, vulnerable, almost petulant, more like a spoiled little boy than the big TV star.

Beneath the drunkenness, Wanda-Jean felt empty and far from satisfied. In bed, he was a long way from a superstar.

The whole evening had been an awful disappointment. Wanda-Jean had imagined he would take her to one of the city's most exclusive restaurants or nightclubs. She had picked out a luxurious white evening gown from the wardrobe that the network had given her when she started on the Dreamroad.

To her amazement Priest had shown up in a faded but well-tailored work suit. He announced that they were going to Old Town.

"Old Town?"

Priest had grinned. "Sure, what's wrong with Old Town?"

"Nothing, but . . ."

"I go over to Old Town a lot. It's one of the few places in town where either you don't get recognized, or the ones who do ain't interested."

Wanda-Jean wasn't too happy about his plan. She had rather wanted to be recognized, particularly with Bobby Priest.

Old Town was, strictly speaking, part of the twilight area. Unlike Lincoln Avenue, which had just been left to decay, Old Town had been cosmeticized into a rather cutesy bohemian neighborhood. It was where poets, painters, and musicians lived side by side with trendy executives who filled their apartments with bric-a-brac from the fifties and sixties and pretended they were nonconformist and artistic.

Wanda-Jean had looked down at her dress with an expression of horror. "I can't go to Old Town dressed like this."

Bobby Priest had laughed. "You can go to Old Town dressed any way you want to."

"With you done up like a truck driver?"

"We'll make a very striking couple, and anyway, there isn't time for you to get changed all over again."

Still protesting, Wanda-Jean had been hustled into the

lift and down to the waiting car. They drove across the
city, alone with just the chauffeur and bodyguard.

Bobby had been right about two things. Nobody had
seemed to recognize them, and nobody took much notice
of Wanda-Jean's overelaborate dress, although she had
still spent most of the evening feeling slightly ridiculous.

One mercy was that the place they went to was very
dark, almost dark enough to forget about the bodyguard
who sat like a squat, broad-shouldered boulder at the
next table.

When you got down to basics, the place was a small,
nondescript cellar. The walls were probably damp but,
mercifully, hidden in the gloom. The decor was a loving, if grubby, re-creation of the beatnik era. The furniture was mismatched. The crowning glory of each table
was a red and white checked tablecloth and a candle stuck
in a wax-encrusted Chianti bottle. These were the only
source of light, except for a couple of spotlights that were
trained on a small stage.

For maybe the first hour, all Wanda-Jean could think
of was why Bobby Priest had brought her to a place like
this. The tables were crammed with an assortment of
standard weirdos. Some were so far into the part that they
sported long lank hair and beards, or black and white
existentialist makeup—what was the name of the chick
who started the whole thing? Juliette something?

The food wasn't all that bad. It had a loose base in
Italian cooking. Wanda-Jean suspected that it was loaded
down with illegal flavorings, and maybe other illegal in-
gredients, as well.

With just about anybody else Wanda-Jean would have
come right out and demanded he explain what he thought
he was doing bringing her to a cruddy place like this.
With Bobby Priest, she just didn't feel able to.

It was made doubly difficult by the fact that somebody
seemed to have hit the man's off button. The stream of
patter appeared to have totally dried. He sat in silence,

pushing food into his mouth with a kind of mechanical enthusiasm. Every now and then he'd pause and tap his fork in time to the resident jazz trio. Conversation was zero. Wanda-Jean had become angry and confused. First of all he'd brought her up to this dump in Old Town, and then he treated her as if she wasn't even there.

Wanda-Jean still hadn't been able to summon up the courage to confront Priest with her displeasure. Instead she fumed inside, and went on drinking the harsh red wine that he had insisted on ordering. The cabaret, if one could call it that, started. The trio vacated the tiny stage, and were replaced by a wild-haired poet who bellowed unintelligible, and frequently obscene, blank verse across the smoke-filled room.

After the poet, a skinny kid with a guitar sat on a stool and, accompanying himself, did an unsuccessful job of reviving the kind of protest music that was popular around the time of the Asian war, a period that even Wanda-Jean's mother was too young to remember.

When the kid finally was through, the trio came back accompanied by a young and not very attractive girl with stringy black hair and makeup like a corpse. She sang one almost inaudible song, then slipped out of her kimono-style robe and, stark naked, proceeded to go through a series of listless but supposedly symbolic gyrations.

Bobby Priest applauded loudly after each act. Wanda-Jean, by the time the dancer came, was slumped, elbows on the table, her chin resting on her fists. For the first time all evening, Priest deigned to notice.

"What's the matter? Don't you like it?"

Wanda-Jean scowled. "This half-assed amateur talent show, what's there to like?"

Priest shrugged. "I can't get enough of it."

The statement had been delivered as though it was an absolute truth. It was enough to make Wanda-Jean sit up straight in her chair.

"You're kidding?"

"Why should I kid?"

Wanda-Jean had looked around the room with almost slack-jawed amazement. "You like . . . this?"

"Sure."

"Jesus Christ, why?"

"I'll tell you . . ."

He hesitated as two women pushed past the table. One was young, in a not very fashionable, but timelessly clinging, red dress with slits up to her hips. She treated Priest to a long liquid stare and puffed sexually on a thin black cigar. The other was at the end of an emaciated, almost cadaverous middle age. Her dress was a vastly expensive couture house creation. A mink stole was thrown around her mottled shoulders. The older woman made a small impatient gesture and they both moved on. None of the regular bearded and work-clothed clientele paid them any attention. Bobby Priest was the single exception. He winked at Wanda-Jean.

"How about those two?"

"How about them?"

"Five gets you ten they're a couple of dykes into S and M. I figure the old one wants to get the young one home and whip her crazy."

Wanda-Jean couldn't help picturing the scene, but she was determined not to be impressed. "So? They looked pretty out of place here."

"You think so?"

"Didn't they?"

"Looked to me like they fitted perfectly."

Wanda-Jean had shaken her head at that point. "I don't understand. I don't understand any of this."

"I expect you figured I was going to take you to some classy downtown joint and we'd wind up in tomorrow's gossip columns, right?"

Wanda-Jean was a little taken aback. "Yes . . . something like that."

"Well, let me tell you something, sister. Let me explain something. You want to know why I come to a dump like this?"

Wanda-Jean nodded. "I'll tell you. This is one of the few places in this whole fucking city where I can go without having people point and stare and elbow each other to get close to me. I need that. I need somewhere where I can be me, where I don't have to be Bobby Priest."

For the very first time Wanda-Jean noticed that, close up, there was something a little mad about Bobby Priest's eyes. The eyes seemed to bore into her.

"You don't understand what I'm talking about, do you?"

Wanda-Jean did her best to look sympathetic. She had decided it was the best way to deal with him. "Sure I understand."

"Bullshit you do. You're just starting on this. I've been on it forever. I've seen a thousand of you come and go. You all run around, getting your kicks out of being somebody for the first time."

"What's wrong with that?"

"There's nothing wrong with it, except I've been somebody so goddamn long I've had it."

Wanda-Jean wasn't sure she could handle this. She wondered what Priest was on. "You don't mean that. You wouldn't go on doing the show if you didn't like it."

"So I don't even get a night off now and then?" He waved his arm around the room. "You see these weirdos here? They don't know from shit about me or you or game shows or feelies, and they care even less. That's what I call a night off."

"I'm sure you need it . . . ."

"But not on your time. You wanted to go to some joint where everyone would recognize us. Right?"

"I didn't say that."

"But it's true."

"I don't want to fight with you." Wanda-Jean was actually scared. It all seemed to be going wrong on her. She couldn't afford to get on the wrong side of Bobby Priest.

"Yeah, well . . ."

To her surprise Priest suddenly slumped. His shoulders sagged. He looked older and much less energetic than before. "I expect you want to go."

It was too fast for Wanda-Jean. "I . . ."

"We'll go back to your hotel."

The totally flat statement was much too fast. Wanda-Jean had expected to wind up in bed with Priest, but she had expected at least some sort of token persuasion. She let out a confused laugh. "Sure, yeah, okay, let's go."

Back at the hotel it had become even stranger. Priest had lapsed into silence again on the ride home. Wanda-Jean had half expected to be taken to the hotel bar for a drink. Instead she was steered straight into the lift and up to her, or rather the network's, suite. The silence continued as they rode up in the lift and went through the living room into the bedroom. The moment they were in the bedroom, Bobby Priest had started taking off his clothes. There hadn't been a word. Something rebelled inside her. There was a limit to everything, even for Bobby Priest. She planted her hands squarely on her hips.

"What the hell do you think you're doing?"

Priest turned and looked at her. His face registered surprise. "I was taking my clothes off. What else?"

"Why?"

"What do you mean, why?"

"What I said, why? You going to take a bath or something?"

"I imagined we were going to fuck."

Wanda-Jean became really angry. "That's what you imagined, did you?"

"Well . . ."

"No sweet talk, no build up, nothing. Just strip off and get to it?''

"What do you want, champagne and flowers?"

"Why the hell not?"

"It all comes to the same thing in the end. Why bother with a whole lot of phony bullshit?"

"Phony or not, at least I get to keep some pride. I get to be more than just something for you to jerk off in. Even hookers get paid."

Priest sneered. "So how much do you want?"

"You bastard!"

"Yeah? Why so worked up, sweetie? Don't make me laugh with all this crap about pride. You lost all your pride when you went in for the show. All you got left is greed. You'd do anything to stay on the show, and as far as you're concerned, I am the show. You screwed everyone you thought might do you the slightest bit of good, so why waltz around?"

He had started to move toward her.

"You might as well just get down. I'm only one more."

He put his hands on her shoulders and pushed her back on the bed. Wanda-Jean was way past resisting. She fell back limply. Priest started tearing at her clothes. A part of her wanted to fight him off, to kick and scratch and hurt him, but the rest of her just couldn't raise the energy.

There has been a certain relief in the fact that it was all over in a flash. Priest came almost as soon as he had started. Wanda-Jean wondered if maybe he got his real kick beforehand. Was he a degradation freak? He lay flat on his back staring at the ceiling in silence. Wanda-Jean gathered up what was left of her clothes and her dignity and and retreated into the bathroom. She felt as though being sick might be an appropriate gesture, but even that seemed a bit futile. Instead, she took a shower and cleaned her teeth. When she returned to the bedroom, Priest was asleep. She slipped into bed. Fortunately, it was so large that there was room for an appreciable space between them.

◇ RALPH HAD DECIDED NOT TO GO HOME. It had been a tense, unhappy day at the vault. There were rumors all over the building, rumors that had even penetrated as deep as the underground dreamworld over which he and Sam presided. There were changes coming. That seemed to be the only point of agreement in the numerous conflicting stories. There was some major reorganization being planned. What exactly that meant was far from clear. Everyone claimed to know the inside scoop. Everyone had the details, but when taken as a whole, all the gossip really added up to was a mass of contradiction and confusion. Some said that there was going to be massive cutbacks and thousands would be thrown out of work. Others whispered that there was going to be equally massive expansion, and that with thousands of new jobs and increased bonuses, happy days were really here. Many responded to that with mutterings of ''Don't hold your breath.'' The worst doomsayers claimed that there was something radically wrong with the entire system, and that the government was going to close down the whole IE operation. Those last claims, however, were made very quietly. To talk about anything like that within the walls of CM and in the places that CM employees gathered was viewed as a clear case of sedition, and although it wasn't actual grounds for dismissal, grounds could be easily found. Needless to say, Ralph feared for his job. Although he cursed it, Ralph's job was everything to him. It was all that stood between him and being absolutely lost in the twilight as just another wino. Sam probably feared, too, but on this particular day, he appeared too doped up even to approach his anxieties.

Ralph had actually started out going for the RT in the usual way, driven by the force of habit. He made it as far as Reagan Plaza when something inside him revolted. He couldn't face the ride; he couldn't face sitting on the slowly emptying train, watching the doors, waiting for some mob of sociopath weirdies to come storming aboard and make him a victim. Without really thinking about it, he stood up as the monorail pulled into Reagan and left the train along with the late shoppers and the executives on their way to the heliport and their comfortable apartments in the security towers that surrounded the plaza. As he came out of the station and walked through the lavish Reagan atrium, he had no real idea where he intended to go, but that soon fell into place. Beyond the Reagan development there was a small enclave of traditional streets with shops and old-style Irish bars. They were not unlike the streets he had known when he was a boy, streets that were reasonably well policed and safe to stroll down without having an obvious reason for being there.

The first bar he came to was an executive hangout, recognizable by its polished brass and hanging plants. He gave the place, ironically called Ralph's, the go by and continued to walk. The next bar he came to, the Saddle Horn, was too dark and gay and noisy for his taste, filled with too many cruising figures briefly illuminated by spinning lasers. He kept on going, enjoying the chance to walk aimlessly, in no hurry to get anywhere. It was another two blocks before he saw what he wanted. The green neon shamrock and the red and white Himmler beer sign glowed like the lights of home in the gathering dusk.

The place was called the Pride of Erin, and the inside

was quite as welcoming as the exterior. It was filled with the comfortable smell of beer and cigarette smoke. When one lived out in the twilight sprawl, it became all too easy to forget what comfort really meant. Sure there were bars along Lincoln Avenue, and they also smelled of beer and cigarettes, but out there, one could never quite get away from the tension, the automatic glance up when a stranger walked in, the ostentation of the antitheft devices on the cash register, and the nagging fear that at any given moment one of the other customers might explode. There was too much poverty out around the bars on Lincoln Avenue. There were always the broken fittings in the bathrooms, and the Christmas decorations that no one had bothered to take down in five or six years. In the Pride of Erin, there were bowls of pretzels on the bar, and the bartender actually smiled at Ralph when he walked in and sat down on a stool.

The bartender was a young kid with slicked-back hair and a tan. "So how's it going?"

Ralph eased the cramps in his shoulders. "Well, I got to tell you, it's been a bitch of a day, but I'm hoping that it'll get better."

The bartender nodded sympathetically. "Maybe a drink would help?"

Ralph grinned. "I didn't come in here for a prayer meeting."

"What'll it be?"

Ralph didn't hesitate. "Scotch and a beer back."

"You want the Jap or the real stuff?"

Ralph had intended to go with Japanese, but then he changed his mind. "Give me the real stuff. Dewars if you've got it."

"We don't have no beer on tap."

"Never mind, nothing's perfect. Give me a bottle of Himmler Light."

The bartender placed Ralph's drinks in front of him

and then pointed to the CM logo on the front of his overalls. "You work for them?"

Ralph nodded. "Sure do."

"You must be doing okay then?"

Ralph grimaced. "Tell me about it."

The bartender seemed genuinely interested. "You work on the feelies?"

Ralph sighed. "It ain't as glamorous as you might think. It's really only a job."

The bartender smiled knowingly. "Yeah, I bet."

Ralph warmed slightly, basking in the third-hand celebrityhood. "Well, you know, every job does have its moments."

The bartender tapped the side of his nose. "You ever meet Connie Starr?"

Ralph laughed. "Stood next to her in an elevator once, but most of the time they keep the stars away from the likes of me."

"So what do you do? Technician or something?"

"Right. I actually work in the client end of the operation, with what we call the stiffs."

"Stiffs?"

"The ones who've signed on for life. The rich folks who just lay there, dreaming they're James Bond or Genghis Khan for the rest of their days. Me and my partner take care of six hundred of them."

"That sounds like some job."

Ralph shook his head. "It's mainly automated. There isn't that much to do. Thank God for the union, that's what I say."

The bartender moved away to serve another customer but came back to Ralph when he was through. Like most people, he was fascinated by the idea of the feelies. "That's got to be the life, though. Spending all of your time living out a fantasy."

Ralph had a thought. Okay, so he wasn't going to blow the whistle on CM. Nobody said that he couldn't start a grassroots rumor. "To tell the truth, we've been having a bit of trouble lately with the longtimers."

The bartender immediately looked interested. "Trouble?"

Ralph looked around to see that no one else was listening, then leaned forward conspiratorially and lowered his voice. "They've been dying on us."

The bartender didn't seem to know if he believed Ralph or not. "Dying?"

"Just passing away."

"I never heard about that."

"Of course you didn't. It's a very closely guarded secret."

"Why are they dying?"

"Nobody knows. It might be a glitch in the equipment, although those Germans don't usually screw up, or it could be that, after a couple of years in a feelie, they just give up and die. It may be that human beings just ain't designed to live like a cactus."

The bartender was shaking his head. "That's pretty freaky. How many have died so far?"

"Not many yet, but I'm afraid it's only the start."

The bartender poured Ralph a shot on the house. "It's one time that I'm glad I'm poor."

Ralph drained the free drink. "Amen to that."

"What are they going to do about it? They can't just let people die."

"Can't they? So far, all they've been doing is keeping it quiet."

"That's terrible."

Ralph sipped his beer. "That's big corporations for you. They just don't give a damn."

"THERE HAVE BEEN, FOR WANT OF A better word, rumors."

Kingsley Deutsch stood at the end of the absurdly long conference table. His stance was dramatic, as was the pause that he left for his opening statement to sink in.

"In fact, the rumors that are circulating in this corporation have reached totally unacceptable levels, levels that can only indicate that morale is approaching a state of instability. Instability at any time is something, gentlemen, that we simply cannot afford. We cannot afford it at any time, but we particularly cannot afford it right now."

The special emergency meeting was being held in the penthouse boardroom, the highest pinnacle of power in Combined Media. The boardroom itself was designed to embody, reflect, and amplify that power. The vast panoramic window behind Deutsch looked out over an expanse of city that stretched out almost to the horizon. The sky was a deep blue with streaks of wispy, pale clouds, planes came and went, and the light of the towers and streets were just starting to come alive.

Outside, everything seemed so normal. In the boardroom, there was a feeling of isolation, almost a sense of impending doom. The pair of huge marble neo-Assyrian godheads that flanked the window and supported the vaulted cathedral ceiling glared angrily down from behind Deutsch at the men and women assembled there as though silently demanding explanations. Deutsch himself looked as though he was also about to demand explana-

165

tions. Kingsley Deutsch wasn't a tall man, but he made up for what he lacked in stature by unrelenting energy. More than once he had been described in the media as Napoleonic. Like Bonaparte, his dress was deliberately understated. His black conservative suit may have been infinitely forgettable, even if it had cost more than three thousand dollars, but there was no forgetting his face. He was not a handsome man, but there were few faces outside of a handful of mass murderers and psychopaths that showed such will and determination. His chin jutted in permanent belligerence; his small blue eyes, beneath knitted, almost invisible brows, were penetrating to the point of being scary. The only touch of vanity was the way in which he compensated for his thinning gray hair with a deep, even tan that seemed to be the main reason behind weekends spent at his tax haven, a Haitian chateau just outside Port au Prince.

"I have called this special meeting because I have an announcement to make that I believe may be of historic proportions."

Kingsley Deutsch didn't mince words. He was a megalomaniac, certainly, but he was an absolutely successful megalomaniac, and if he said historic proportions, he meant historic proportions. Historic as in history, not historic as in a fifteen-second sound bite on the next day's news shows. The men and women who had been summoned to the penthouse stood transfixed, and the pause before he continued was a form of torture. The torture, however, wasn't about to stop.

"Before the announcement, though, I think we have to spend a little time taking stock of the situation that currently exists within this enterprise of ours. There is little point attempting to advance into history if we cannot summon even the confidence to face tomorrow. I said that this corporation was beset by rumor. Your comments please."

The frightening blue eyes scanned the assembled men and women. There were just ten of them, so small an assembly that they were dwarfed by the overwhelming conference table that was almost thirty feet of dark mahogany polished to the finish of glass. For ten people, however, they wielded a great deal of power. They were the ten department heads, the ten top people in the whole of Combined Media. Between then, they commanded almost, although not quite, as much power as Deutsch himself. And yet, they said nothing. The meeting itself already had them off balance. It had been the end of the working day when they had been summoned without warning to Deutsch's presence: "The penthouse. Immediately."

Deutsch looked around once more and half smiled. Behind him, hanging over the city, a skyboard advertising Pepsi Cola had lit up. He focused on Madison Renfield.

"What about you, Madison? You're our hero of the glib."

Renfield raised his hands in a somewhat helpless gesture. "There are always rumors, Kingsley. It'd be unhealthy for a corporation to be without rumors in this day and age. Let's face it, the ways of the modern corporation are a little Byzantine."

Deutsch raised his eyebrow. "Byzantine, Madison?"

Renfield had the expression of a man who had very little left to lose. "Byzantine, Kingsley."

Deutsch smiled. "So, Madison, do you see me as a Byzantine emperor?"

"I wouldn't volunteer the analogy."

Deutsch looked at the other nine. "Madison may, in fact, be right, but let us remember one thing. The Byzantine emperor could rule only according to the information that he received. He was frequently only as good as his intelligence, and that was only if his intelligence was untainted. One of Adolf Hitler's greatest problems was that he surrounded himself with individuals who told him only what he wanted to hear. That's not only bad intelligence but criminally unintelligent. I have, throughout my long career, taken great care to see that my own intelligence sources were as direct and pure as I could make them.''

That, also, was no exaggeration. Deutsch was famous for his elaborate spy system, which seemed to extend to every level of the corporation despite all the efforts of the individual departments to suppress, filter, and regulate stories that went up to the penthouse.

''During the last few days, these sources have been telling me a great many things. So many things, in fact, that the sheer volume of information that I have been receiving recently would be enough on its own to cause me a measure of alarm. Let me enumerate some of the things I've been hearing.''

The ten heads of department were no longer transfixed. They were now preparing to squirm in their leather chairs with the CM logo embossed in gold on the backs. No one could remember when Kingsley Deutsch had called a meeting that promised so much discomfort. It was quite usual for him to call individual department heads onto the carpet, but to summon them en masse for a dressing down was quite unprecedented.

''Now, where shall I start? Perhaps with the phenomenon of client death that, although substantively a closely guarded corporation secret, seems to have become widely talked about.''

Gorges Gomez of Client Services and Renfield of PR exchanged worried glances. Deutsch caught the exchange.

''You have something to say? Something to add to the discussion?''

Gomez cleared his throat nervously. ''There are a lot of rank and file workers who know about this. Many of them are employed only because of the concessions that were made to the union in the original charter. It is virtually impossible to silence so many people whose company loyalty may at best be tenuous.''

Renfield jumped in. "I think the important thing is that we have been extremely successful at keeping even a hint of this from the media—"

Deutsch waved him to silence. "Just relax. This is not a court of inquiry. I am merely conducting an informal review of some of our current problems. All will become clear when, following this review, I make my promised announcement. All I want to do now is to bring some matters out into the open that have previously been the preserve of locked doors and whispered conversations, matters like, for instance, the reason that two of my most senior executives should meet in a public restaurant to discuss the reestablishment of death experience research."

Edouard Hayes went white. His face took on a strangled expression.

Deutsch looked directly at him. "You have something you want to add?"

"I . . . really must make it clear that Vallenti and I were only discussing the possibilities that some clandestine group might be attempting to start up such research again. After Jonas's research and the resulting prostitute murders when he went insane—"

Deutsch held up a hand. "How many times do I have to tell you that this is not an inquiry?"

He walked slowly down the length of the table. In the middistance, outside the panoramic window, the skyboard was flashing the current Pepsi slogan in red, white, and blue holotype.

Another Generation
Another Generation
Another Generation

"Ladies and gentlemen, it would appear that we are spending too much of our time reflecting on thoughts of death. The death of clients, the death experience, perhaps these are a cover for a deeper unease about the basic philosophy behind what we are doing. It's there in our own vernacular. We refer to our clients as 'stiffs,' to the standard IE unit as a 'coffin.' Could it be that we subconsciously feel that, in marketing a technological discorporate fantasy, we have become vendors of a form of death? That is a question that you may find answered sooner than you think. Before that happens, however, I cannot impress upon you more strongly that this is absolutely the wrong time for this question to be asked. An army that broods upon death through the eve of battle is not going to win any place in history. Unless they are defending the Alamo. Has Combined Media become the Alamo, gentlemen? If it has, I have to warn you. You may have to start thinking of me as your personal Santa Ana.''

◆ THE PRIDE OF ERIN WAS STARTING TO fill up, and Ralph's money was definitely dwindling. He had never been the kind who could nurse a single drink through half the evening. He drank up and ordered again. When he couldn't order any more it was time to get the hell out of wherever he was. Also, he was no longer feeling comfortable in the place. There were couples meeting up for dates, junior execs in sweatpants hot from the raquets court, and women who had been working late now, with their blouses unfastened a couple of notches, looking for fun. Ralph knew perfectly well that sitting in his overalls, three parts drunk, he had nothing that represented any approximation of their idea of fun. God, it had been so long since he had been with a woman. He really didn't need the reminder. He finished his drink, nodded to the barman, and headed for the door.

There was nothing left to do but return to the RT and make the ride out to Lincoln Avenue. He had been a damn fool to go looking for that bar. It was starting to get late, and even the monorail would be doubly dangerous.

As he walked through Reagan Płaza, he noticed that a fairly large crowd had gathered in front of the Sanyo-Hyatt. Using any excuse to put off boarding the train for as long as possible, he sauntered in the direction of the big modern hotel to investigate.

It wasn't the usual crowd that he would have expected to find in Reagan Plaza. They were mainly blue collar like himself, welfare cases, even, and a sprinkling of definite oddities. A lot of them carried cameras; he saw autograph books, and a bearded individual in a ragged suit of the executive style of five years earlier was holding up a placard that read YOU ARE DOOMED! There had to be some major celebrity staying inside. He ambled up to a woman in a blue coat who looked very unhappy to be way in the back of the crowd. Ralph smiled at her, doing his best to look every inch the amiable drunk.

"What's going on?"

"I'm not going to be able to see."

"What's there to see?"

The woman in the blue coat looked at him as though he were crazy. " 'Wildest Dreams.' "

"Huh?"

"The contestants are coming out, and I ain't going to see them."

"No shit."

"Would you help me get through?"

"Jesus, I don't know."

Ralph took a closer look at the crowd. They weren't in front of the main entrance to the hotel; police sawhorses and squads of uniformed officers held them back on the sidewalk at either side, so they wouldn't get in the way of the guests coming in and out. The cops controlling the crowd seemed to be treating the whole event as fairly routine, although Ralph did notice that there was a large, black, unmarked armored truck of the kind used by the CRAC squad parked across the street.

"The contestants for 'Wildest Dreams' stay here?"

"Don't you know nothing?"

Ralph blinked. "Apparently not."

"So will you help me through to the front?"

Ralph looked at the woman for the first time. She wasn't really bad-looking in a washed-out kind of way. She really could be quite attractive if one could get past the shabby nylon utility coat. He reminded himself that he was no raving prize. "Maybe we could ease ourselves a little closer. How soon do the contestants come out?"

"It's only the Dreamroad contestants. Bobby Priest himself is with them sometimes."

Ralph was a little bemused. There was a definite light of obsession in the woman's eyes. Even the obsessed could be grateful after the fact. "How soon do they come out?"

"Any minute."

Ralph put a protective arm around her and started easing them deeper into the crowd. The "Wildest Dreams" fans didn't part easily, and Ralph had to use some degree of applied pressure. He received a few threats and curses for his pains. All of the "Wildest Dreams" fans seemed to be equally desperate and equally obsessed. How could anyone get that way about a goddamned game show? There was a definite tension in the crowd, but there was also a lonely, unhappy feeling, as well. These people seemed to take little pleasure in what they were doing. Ralph knew drunks like that. He and the woman in the blue coat did make some progress, though, and came within four layers of the front before they were stopped by the pressure of bodies. He still had his arm around the woman's shoulders, and since she didn't ask him to take it away, he left it there.

There was shouting at the front rows. The woman in the blue coat stiffened.

"They're coming! They're coming!"

She started bouncing up and down, making small squeaking noises. Ralph realized that it was the same thing that contestants did when they won big on the greed shows like "Hundred Thousand Giveaway." And she wasn't the only one. The whole crowd was pushing and jumping. The situation suddenly felt very unstable, and Ralph realized that it was about the last place in the world that a drunk needed to be. He had to fight for his footing as the crowd surged sideways. He still had his arm around her and couldn't get it free. The whole mob was pressing forward as though some very, very stupid collective mind was brutishly determined to push its way through the police lines. Ralph stumbled again. He let go of the woman. There was chaos up ahead. People were screaming. It was hard to tell if it was hysteria or pain. One of the barriers seemed to have collapsed, and people had gone down with it. There were people on the sidewalk. They were being trampled. He almost lost his footing as he stumbled into one of the ones who had fallen. He went down himself a moment later, but was able to struggle up again. The two people who went down in front of him and cushioned his fall were not so lucky. He started pushing backward against the tide, trying to ease over to the wall of the hotel. At least he would have his back to something. He had to get out of this bloody insanity.

THE MEETING IN THE PENTHOUSE boardroom of Combined Media continued. It seemed destined to go on all night. It had moved into its second phase. Deutsch was cross-questioning each department head in turn, dragging out corporate secrets that they never would have willingly revealed to other departments. Covert glances were being exchanged, and there was real fear in the room. Either something earth-shaking was coming, or Deutsch had gone stone mad. Right at that moment it was the turn of Charlotte Estes, the head of Research. Deutsch stood behind her, lightly resting his hands on the back of her chair.

"So, Charlotte, to clarify, according to your research, there would appear to be no way to predict which clients will succumb to premature death syndrome. You're saying that some will die after a couple of years, while others will last out their full natural span."

Estes shook her head. "There's really no such thing as a natural span in the IE dreamstate. Of the twenty test subjects that we have been monitoring since the start of public availability, one died after seven months. Three more went in the third year, and a fourth one a year later. One died four months ago, and two more went in the last three weeks. The others are still alive, but they show distinct signs of premature aging. I see no chance of them surviving beyond another five years."

Gorges Gomez leaned forward in his chair. "You mean you knew about the probablility of premature death all along?"

"We suspected it."

"And no one was warned?"

Deutsch took over. "What would you have had us do, Gorges? Shut down the entire service and go into liquidation?"

Gomez shook his head. "No, but . . ."

Madison Renfield half raised a hand. "Perhaps I might assist here."

Deutsch smiled. "The floor is yours, Madison."

"We in Public Relations have done a little research of our own on the matter of PDS."

Gomez muttered under his breath. "When the shit turns nasty, call it by its initials."

Deutsch fixed him with a cold stare. "You have something to add, Gorges?"

Gomez shook his head sadly. "No, Kingsley, not a thing."

Deutsch turned to Renfield. "Please go on."

"Well, to boil it down to basics, all the research that we've done on lifespan clients seems to demonstrate that, once they've entered the program, no one on the outside gives a damn about them. As far as the world is concerned, they've gone down a one-way street and aren't coming back. Beneath this there is also a measurable level of resentment. The lifespan client is perceived to have committed an act of terminal selfishness, and what happens to them from there on in is strictly their own problem."

Throughout the meeting, David Patel of Legal had been making periodic notes on a yellow pad. Now he looked up questioningly. "Was this attitude research conducted only in terms of the public at large, or was there a specific survey of friends and families of those who became lifespan clients?"

Renfield smiled. He was ahead of that question. "It combined both. We discovered that among the families of longtimers, there was frequently a good deal of relief mingled with the resentment. All too often they were getting rid of a relative who was proving to be a liability of one kind or another.''

Edouard Hayes frowned. ''The fact that the stiff's family didn't like him isn't going to stop them bringing a lawsuit for some hundred million or so if he drops dead in our care.''

Patel looked at Hayes as though he was stating the childishly obvious. ''The original charter covers us against this kind of eventuality. The lifespan client basically renounces most of his or her civil rights when they enter the program. As far as the law is concerned, they are legally dead. Their assets are held in trust or disposed of just as in the event of death, and they have no estate as such on which claims can be made. Our only legal responsibility is to see that the clients don't cause harm to the living. It would take an act of Congress to change our position.''

Charlotte Estes looked up with a grin. ''I take it we have nothing to fear from Congress.''

Deutsch also smiled. ''We have made a considerable investment over the years to insure that we have nothing to fear from Congress.''

He walked back to the head of the table.

''While we are indulging in this almost Maoist exercise in confession and self-criticism, there is something that I should perhaps bring out into the light. A number of you seem to be concerned that—how did you put it, Edouard?—'a clandestine group within the corporation' was attempting to revive death experience research. I see that I must look to my own security.''

Edouard Hayes stared at Deutsch openmouthed. ''Your security, Kingsley?''

''I authorized the monitoring of that execution down in Mississippi.''

There were ten stunned faces around the conference table. Since the failure of the initial research, the monitoring of an actual death, on Deutsch's specific personal instructions, had been the most taboo act in all of Combined Media. That Deutsch himself should have secretly authorized such a thing was unthinkable.

"You look surprised. Did you think that, just because Jonas went insane, the whole subject of humanity's greatest mystery should be shelved forever? I waited until I was confident that the dust had settled sufficiently and then I made my move. It is, after all, the ultimate curiosity. Did you really think that I would resist it?"

It was Charlotte Estes who asked the obvious question. "Have you experienced the recording?"

Deutsch shook his head. "Not yet. I have never seen myself as a human guinea pig. There is another set of convicts who are, as we speak, being exposed to the experience. If no harmful effects are revealed, I will experience the recording myself. After that, I will decide on our next move."

Renfield leaned back in his chair. "Is that the announcement?"

Deutsch laughed. "Oh, no, Madison. That was just a minor confession. My announcement is something else again."

◇ BY THE TIME THEY HAD REACHED THE foyer, it had all become very brisk. Wanda-Jean, the other three Dreamroad contestants, and Bobby Priest were surrounded on all sides by a loose phalanx of aides, network bodyguards, and hotel security. Wanda-Jean felt as though she was riding on a wave of nervous excitement. She wasn't sure whether her nerves or her excitement were the stronger. On one hand she was about to go through the tension and thoroughly degrading exposure of another show. On the other, being in the middle of this small, urgent crowd of men in dark suits and uniforms made her feel wanted and important.

Heads turned as they came out of the elevators. The entourage closed up as they made their way past the long reception desk, the deep armchairs, the hanging plants, and the small fountain. Although people stared there was no other response inside the hotel. The customers of the Sanyo Hyatt had too much credit to get in an uproar over TV celebrities. Outside on the street, however, it was a whole different thing. Cops and more hotel security men were holding back a milling, pushing mob that filled the entire pavement in front of the hotel.

The "Wildest Dreams" party hesitated just inside the automatic glass doors of the hotel. Two limousines drew up outside. The cops had their clubs out, and were only with difficulty keeping the crowd off the cars. Wanda-Jean stared at the surging crush in horror. For the first time since she had been involved with the game show, she was physically frightened. She looked at the nearest security man in some alarm.

"Why don't they take us out through the back way? Won't it save all this trouble and fuss?"

"I think they like the fuss, sweetheart. They figure it's good for business."

A police sergeant, just outside the glass doors, signaled to the squad inside. The doors opened, and everyone moved out. The first few steps were slow and tentative. Then they hit the air and it started in earnest. The security formed into a flying wedge. They were off and running, hands clutched. She was swamped by the noise of the crowd but, at the same time, couldn't make out a word they were saying. She couldn't even judge their mood. Did they hate her or love her? Were they grabbing at her to show their affection or tear her apart? The fingers were clawed, the faces were distorted. They slammed into the cops with furious, violent determination to get through. They seemed unwilling to give up, even when the cops moved in with clubs swinging.

There was a brief moment when Wanda-Jean thought they were going to get to her. Then the broad back of a network man moved into her line of vision as he put himself in the way of the rush. A middle-aged woman, with two-tone orange and pink hair and inch-thick makeup, howled something before a cop grabbed her and swung her bodily away. Absurdly, Wanda-Jean had a picture of her open mouth imprinted, almost photographically, on her memory. There had been flecks of orange lipstick on her teeth.

They were almost to the cars and out of the worst of it. A teenage girl tried to duck under a cop's arm. He seized her by the hair but, in so doing, left a space for a short chubby figure of undecided sex to force its way through. It had thick, moist, sagging lips set in a bland, doughy, piggy-eyed face.

It held a plastic spiral-bound book in its hands. It opened this as though offering it to Wanda-Jean for inspection and dropped to its knees. Wanda-Jean had to stop dead to keep herself from falling over it. For a fleeting instant, she had a good look at the inside of the book. It was crammed with pictures of her, pictures of Wanda-Jean, presumably taken from a TV set. They showed her in the most contorted, obscene, and humiliating poses.

Wanda-Jean knew there must be people who did bizarre obsessive things because of some celebrity fixation. It just seemed incredible it could be done to her. She was totally spooked for a second. What else were people doing? She jerked away and collided with a bodyguard. She was lifted off her feet and virtually thrown in the back of one of the waiting cars. She fell in a heap on Brigitte and another contestant. The door slammed. She saw the kneeling figure bowled over by a headlong rush. Both he and his book of pictures were trampled underfoot. Hands

beat on the windows and roof of the car. The driver
gunned it away. Everyone was jerked into the back of the
seats. They were wrapped in the smell of old leather.
Almost miraculously they broke free of the crowd. Ahead
of them a police car with three sets of sirens broke up
the downtown traffic.

Wanda-Jean pulled herself up and peered out of the car
window. People on the sidewalk were stopping to stare
at them as they raced past with their police escort. At
least she was going to the show in style.

RALPH WAS HURLED BODILY AGAINST A
plate glass window; it didn't shatter. Right in
front of him a man was being clubbed to the
ground. The woman in the blue coat had vanished. The
CRAC squad was out of their van, employing the only
answer they had to any kind of disturbance, which was
to break heads. On the other side of the glass, rich folk
were drinking cocktails and eating an early dinner before
taking in a show. They stared in blank amazement at the
violence on the sidewalk. Ralph was only two feet from
a fat woman who had frozen in shock with a forkful of
creamcake halfway to her mouth. There was only the
shock of the unexpected in the drinkers' and diners'
faces. There was no real concern or outrage. What was
going on beyond the glass might as well have been happening to another species on another world.

Ralph slid along the window toward a doorway that
would afford a minimal protection. He rolled into it. The
violence was streaming past him. People were running,
shrieking, doing anything to get away from the clubs of

the police. Two CRAC officers grabbed a woman and dragged her off to the van. The only mercy was that, so far, they hadn't used gas. Suddenly there was a helmeted, gas-masked cop in front of his doorway. Seeing Ralph, he raised his club.

Ralph cringed. "Don't hurt me! Don't hurt me!"

The cop paused and lowered the club. "Get out of there!"

Ralph ducked past the cop, who shoved him roughly. Ralph started running. He didn't look back. He ran blindly with the rest, sharing their terror. There were cops in front of the RT station—there would be no refuge in there. Then he was in the atrium, along with a number of others. He looked back. There were no cops in sight. He spotted the woman in the blue coat. She was walking around in a daze. There was blood on her face from a cut forehead. Ralph hurried over to her.

"Are you alright?"

The woman looked at him in complete mystification. It was only after a number of seconds that recognition dawned. "It's you."

"Right."

"You helped me through the crowd."

"Are you okay?"

"Why did they have to do that?"

"You're bleeding."

The woman put a hand to her forehead. She looked surprised at the blood on her fingers. "I'm bleeding."

"You want to go to the emergency room?"

She shook her head emphatically. "I don't like those places."

"You ought to get someone to look at that cut."

"It'll be alright. What I'd really like is a drink."

Despite himself, Ralph grinned. "Now you're talking."

△△△ "OKAY, SO YOU WIN AGAIN."

Sam put down *The House at Pooh Corner* and reached for the TV's on/off switch. The cat watched him with absorbed interest. A picture spread out across the screen. The color shimmered for a moment and then held steady. It was much too green, but Sam didn't bother to adjust it. He didn't really like watching TV. To be precise, he didn't like to have to concentrate on it. Most of the time he would turn it on and just let the sound and vision wash over him. With that attitude, it didn't matter whether the color was balanced or not. He frequently told himself he only turned it on for the sake of the cat. In fact, when Max wasn't eating or pestering Sam in order to eat, he was asleep. Sam attributed a great deal to Max. Much of it was his own imagination.

"So remember, with Securicare, you know who's there."

It was an ad for a closed-circuit door scanner. The scene was a spick, orderly B+ home. A trim, attractive housewife responded to a set of door chimes. The picture cut to the exterior of the same house. Standing on the doorstep was a sinister figure. He wore the typical close-cropped hair, earring, the black nylon jacket and heavy boots of a kid from a welfare gang. He wasn't, however, built like any juvenile Sam had ever seen. He had the physique of a block position ball player. His eyes were red-rimmed and a scar ran down his left cheek. Between thick chubby fingers he held a length of boat chain. He was every B+'s nightmare of rape, robbery, and terror.

Sam looked at Max the cat. "They sure do run some crap."

Max yawned. The picture was back to the housewife. The music held its breath as, unaware of the horror on the step, her hand went to the door latch. Then the picture froze.

"With Securicare you don't have to open to look."

The motion continued again, only the scene had subtly changed. This time the woman's hand was operating the control of a Securicare door scanner. The brute on the step appeared on the machine's small, full color screen. Without hesitation or even any noticeable change of expression, the woman reached for the hall phone, presumably to call for either help or the police. Again the picture froze.

"With Securicare, you know who's there."

Sam sighed. "I guess we don't need one of those. We don't have anything worth stealing."

The NCC logo came up on the screen. The voice over it was urgent. "Tomorrow at ten."

It was a trailer. A gang of gaunt men, clad in filthy rags and holding makeshift weapons, charged across a bare, sunlit expanse of concrete. Another set of men waited for them in a disciplined half circle. They wore tight black uniforms and visored helmets. They all cradled riot guns or held electric prods at the ready. The ragged mob halted. In the middle of them was a pneumatic blonde in a white plastic nurse's outfit. She was obviously a captive or hostage. Her arms were being forced behind her back and the front of her blouse was ripped to fully expose one breast. There was a close-up of one of the men holding her. He yelled, showing a set of yellow, broken teeth.

"You better let us through, Molloy, or the nurse gets it."

A cold voice came from behind a visor. "She knows

she's been on her own since you animals grabbed her.
I'm going to count to five and open fire.''

There was a shot of the riot guns slowly being leveled.

''One—two—three—four.''

Fade-out. The voice-over came back.

''Don't miss May Marsh in another savage episode of
'Penal Colony,' tomorrow at ten, on this channel.''

The NCC logo came back again, only this time it was
against a background of shifting, moving patterns of
color. They were similar to the ones in the feelie adverts.
Loud rock music on the polite side of tension, the kind
the old folks liked, fought with a burst of almost hysterical canned applause. After a few seconds, the music
won. It was joined by an enthusiastic but disembodied
choir.

> ''Everybody's dreaming
> Everybody's scheming
> Everybody's got their
> Wildest dreams
> Maybe it's you
> Baby it's you
> Maybe your wildest dreams
> Really will
> come
> tr-u-u-e.''

A heavenly staircase materialized among the swirling
patterns. The choir was replaced by an equally enthusiastic voice-over.

''And now . . . the man who makes it happen . . . the
man who makes dreams come true . . . Mister . . . Bob
. . . bee . . .''

Sam hit the channel selector. As he flicked through the
seemingly endless selection he looked regretfully at Max.
''I'm sorry, cat. I can't watch those game shows anymore, not since Ralph explained how they were fixed.''

BOBBY PRIEST'S VOICE HAD DROPPED to its lowest, most reverent tone. The crowd were hushed. They weren't going to mess up the moment of anticipation. The light had shrunk to harmonize with the mood. He stood alone in a single white-blue spot. The black sequins on his formal suit glittered with every slight movement.

"Well, my friends, now we come to that moment in the show where the hopes are highest and the pitfalls are deepest."

He paused to let the spurious drama of the moment sink right home.

"Waiting outside are four young people. For each one it is another moment of truth on the trail of their wildest dreams. Very soon you and I will know whether each one of them has come closer to that big prize, that lifetime contract for a feelie of their choice, or whether those dreams will have been dashed forever."

If anyone had cared, right then, to drop a pin, the whole studio would have heard it.

"Yes, my friends, it's that moment again. It's time for . . ." His voice lifted. "The Dreamroad!"

Right on cue the lights blazed up, the audience roared, and Wanda-Jean and her three companions bounced out into the studio. Wanda-Jean made every effort to look as happy and confident as the others. Inside, she felt like a Christian trotting out to meet the lions.

The contestants wore the usual costumes. The only change was that the numbers on them were in gold rather than red as they had been in the preliminary stages.

185

Wanda-Jean didn't doubt they were still made out of the material that inevitably dissolved in water.

Bobby Priest's voice rose over the shouting and cheering of the crowds in the bleachers. The contestants formed a line beside the host's raised podium. Priest turned toward them with a sweeping gesture.

"And let's meet the people who are taking a chance on the chance of a lifetime tonight."

The cameras moved in on the contestants. They all smiled just like they'd been told at the briefing.

"Wearing number one, it's the fantastic Sammy. Those of you who watched last week will remember just how truly amazing Sammy's been on the Dreamroad. If he gets through tonight he's got just two . . ."

He let the momentous fact sink in.

"That's right, two more shows between him and the big, big prize."

The cheering rose to an almost deafening volume. Sammy was the current blue-eyed boy of the show. He had the kind of soft sandy hair that just begged to be tousled, and his open freckled face had inspired double page pin-ups in the fan rags. Sammy ducked his head shyly and gave out a toothy grin as the camera pulled him into close-up. The subteen girls in the crowd went even wilder. Bobby Priest let them run on for a while and then raised his hands to cut it off.

"Okay, okay, that's Sammy. Next to him is Goldie. Goldie's a newcomer, but I'm sure you all remember her from the early rounds. If her luck holds, I'm sure we'll be seeing a lot more of her."

Goldie came on cute to the camera. She was blonde, petite, and came on cute to everyone, particularly Bobby Priest. Wanda-Jean reflected acidly that she might not be so cute to him once he'd had a go at her.

"Wearing number three, the girl who doesn't let anyone get in her way. That's right, it's Wanda-Jean!"

A roar went up from the crowd. At best it could only

be described as jovially hostile. Wanda-Jean sneered at the camera. If they were hell bent on forcing her into this bad girl role, she might as well go along with it.

"And finally, wearing number four, another newcomer starting on the Dreamroad. Let's hear it for Marty."

Since she wasn't so familiar to the crowd, the greeting was only lukewarm. The girl had an angular body and close-cropped dark hair. Wanda-Jean had decided, the first time that she saw her, that Marty was probably a dyke.

Bobby Priest looked serious. "And now we've met the contestants, let's get down to the game."

As on every show, Wanda-Jean and the others had been given the details of the game the previous day. It was a rough one.

"In tonight's game, the contestants won't be playing against one another, they'll be playing against the clock. It's possible that we'll see all four stay on the trail, or it's just as possible that every single contestant will get knocked out!"

He put particular emphasis on the last two words. While he was talking, the players were cued to start walking toward the four clear plastic cylinders, about ten feet high, that were the focal point of the whole studio.

In the front of the cylinders were small, flush-fitting doors of the same material. The ever-present, silver-clad attendants moved in to open them. Each contestant stepped inside a cylinder. The doors were closed behind them. Bobby Priest once again took over the screen.

"The contestants are in position."

The game was a rough one. With the doors sealed, the cylinders started to fill with water. As they slowly filled, the contestants had to solve a problem. They had to re-arrange a set of colored squares into a set pattern they had to guess for themselves. It was a race of mind against rising water.

"Then we'll begin."

Wanda-Jean looked at the arrangement of squares. There were at least two hundred of them, set in a square form. The squares were evenly divided into red, blue, yellow, green, black, and white. They interlocked on a tongue and groove system. There were enough empty spaces to allow them to be maneuvered vertically and horizontally, but not removed from the frame.

The floor under Wanda-Jean's bare feet was already covered with a quarter-inch layer of water, and she hadn't even made a move.

To guess at the correct pattern of colors and then move the squares to conform with it seemed an almost impossible task to complete before the water rose up to her chin.

Wanda-Jean put out a tentative hand. Along the top of the frame that enclosed the whole puzzle was a set of colored lights. There were fifteen of them, one for each vertical row of squares. At the start of the game the lights were all dead. When the particular row was arranged in the correct order, the light came on. It was the players' most valuable aid; in fact, it was their only one.

Wanda-Jean started quickly to rearrange the first row. She had made up her mind, at rehearsal, that there was no point in making a blind guess at the overall pattern. The way she had decided to work was to keep switching squares, one line at a time, until the light came on.

The trouble was that it didn't seem to be working. She frantically shifted the squares of plastic, but the water was already up to her ankles and not even the first light had come on.

This was the game that had cost "Wildest Dreams" its only fatality. A player could go on trying to solve the problem until the water finally forced him or her to float to the top of the cylinder and climb out in disgrace and failure. In order to stay on the Dreamroad, all the contestant had to do was get the right answer. One guy, some eight months earlier, had hung on so doggedly, trying to find the solution, that he'd drowned.

The water was almost up to her knees, when, totally unexpectedly, the first light came on. As Wanda-Jean started on the second line she flashed on the fact that the law of averages wasn't doing her any favors.

The only consolation of the game was that it didn't allow Wanda-Jean any time to think. The only thing that distracted her from total concentration on the little plastic squares was the water slowly creeping up her legs.

The water had started to eat away at the crotch of her costume when the second light came on. Wanda-Jean started on the third row, blessing the merciful release that inside the cylinder the noise of the crowd wasn't audible.

Out of the corner of her eye she could see them. By the time the water had eaten away her suit right up to where the tops of her buttocks curved in to meet her spine, the crowd was on its feet, waving and gesticulating. The third light had not come on yet. Wanda-Jean refused to admit that the game had become, in logical terms, hopeless.

Because of the water, she was now naked from the waist down. They had not bothered to heat the water. It was stone cold. It was hard to know whether the chill clutching at her stomach was the knowledge that she was going to lose or simply the chill of the rising water. There was a cameraman down in the floor in front of her with a handheld camera. He was shooting up at her. She couldn't see a monitor, but she could imagine the shot. There was no way she was going to recover from the humiliation of hundreds of millions of people seeing her like this. The water was creeping up to her breasts. She started to panic. She couldn't concentrate on the puzzle. She had to get out. She had to get away from the lights and the cameras and the howling crowd. The water was up to her neck. The last shred of her costume floated away, rapidly dissolving. She would drown before she would crawl naked in front of them. And then the water was coming up over her chin.

"Noooooo!"

She grabbed for a handhold to haul herself out. There was nothing left.

"WE ARE GOING TO BEGIN THE economy-class program. In one month we will announce a major technological breakthrough that will make IE available to everyone. Ladies and gentlemen, we are about to offer the feelies to the underclass. In a short while, the primary purpose of this endeavor will be in motion."

There had been shocks in the penthouse boardroom all through the meeting—but nothing like this. The heads of department were silent. It was what they always theoretically worked for, but they had never expected it so soon.

Lars Axton, the head of Procurement, was the first one to find his voice. "Is it possible?"

Deutsch nodded. "I believe so."

"The plant involved alone . . ."

"I have had discussions with the president of Krupp. He thinks that his people can handle the production end."

"But there's been no breakthrough."

"And the system was never expensive in the first place. The prices have always been artifically inflated."

Gorges Gomez was shaking his head. "We'll be inundated."

Deutsch smiled. "I'm not saying that we can do everything straightaway. In the beginning, there will be quotas and waiting lists, but those will only excite demand. It will be a year or more until we can offer life contracts to the poor, but we will be receiving considerable, if somewhat covert, financial help from the government.''

Renfield frowned. ''Why should the government . . .''

''Because the government is well aware that what we are basically offering is a painless alternative to the death by disease or starvation of hundreds of millions of people. The feelies provide a safety valve, a place to warehouse the excess population. The cost of maintaining a human being in a feelie fantasy is only cents per day, far less even than the most minimal welfare. Population control by birth control has failed. We have to face that. What we also have to face is that any species that is unable to regulate its birthrate becomes subject to regulation by death in one form or another. Either by plague or by famine or by killing one another. The system is self-selecting. Those who desire nothing more than to live in a garish fantasy will be allowed to do so.''

Deutsch permitted himself a smile. ''And believe me, my friends, the fantasies will become exceedingly garish.''

Renfield sighed. ''I can believe it.''

Deutsch ignored him. ''Those who remain in the real world will be those who are able to accept reality for what it is. We are using technology to reassert a very fundamental Darwinism. We may be giving humanity another chance. In fact, we may well be the last, best hope.''

Deutsch paused to let that sink in.

''Do you now see that, when we are on the brink of something as immense as this, the last thing that we can afford to have is an Alamo state of mind?''

Gorge Gomez was looking exceedingly disturbed ''This is more like Auschwitz than the Alamo.''

Deutsch's eyes narrowed. ''Is that what you believe Gorge?''

"We are talking about marketing a product that we know full well will kill the users in five to seven years. Is that mankind's last best hope?"

"We aren't forcing anyone to do anything. Anyone who enters the fantasy is doing it of their own free will."

"But we'll be concealing the long-term effects. They'll be making the choice without full knowledge of the facts."

"The facts, Gorge? Do any of us ever have full knowledge of the facts? Perhaps these people are merely exchanging duration of life for quality of life. Can you look at it that way, Gorge?"

WANDA-JEAN MOVED LIKE A ZOMBIE. She was trying not to see her cramped little apartment. The only way to hold back the truth that she was back there was simply not to see it. It was the only way to hold back the much more awful truth that the adventure was over. Her pill box was clutched tightly in her hand.

It was like slow motion. Keeping her back very straight, she sank to the floor and crossed her legs. She placed the box very carefully in front of her. She inspected it for a while, then she opened it and tipped the contents out on the floor. The collection had grown considerably since she had been on the show.

With painful method, she began to arrange the pills in neat rows, five to a row. By the time she had finished there were twelve of them, sixty pills. She had been hoarding them since she had started on the show. She studied the pattern of colors formed by the different medications. With infinite patience she started to rearrange them, until she realized that she was echoing the terrible game.

She didn't want to think about it. She stood up and went into the kitchen. She looked in the fridge. It was almost empty, just a piece of aging cheese and a container of Coke. She took the Coke out and went back into the lounge. Her next stop was at the booze cabinet. That too was thinly populated. About an inch and a half remained in a bottle of Jap whiskey.

Wanda-Jean resumed her cross-legged position on the floor. She set the whiskey and the Coke beside the box and pills. She had forgotten a glass. Almost impatiently she went and fetched one, and quickly squatted on the floor again. It was the first time she had moved rapidly since she had left the studio.

The bastards had let her go home in a taxi. They hadn't even bothered to . . .

She wasn't going to think about that. She unscrewed the top of the whiskey bottle. She one third filled the glass. Next she stripped the seal from the Coke container and topped it up. She tasted it experimentally. She added a little more Coke. She tasted it again, and seemed satisfied.

She picked up the first pill, turned it over in her fingers, and put it in her mouth. She sipped her drink and swallowed.

She took a second pill and then a third. She started to get into a kind of mindless rhythm. She took the pills in scrupulous order, up one row and down the next. Pick up the pill, place it on her tongue, sip Jap and Coke, repeat the process.

She had worked her way through a third of them when she started to feel sick and a little dizzy. They couldn't be coming on so fast. It had to be her imagination. She got a grip on herself and pressed on.

The pills were half gone. The nausea had not faded.

She forced down five at once. She couldn't hold it together anymore. Her hand started to shake. She couldn't get herself to control it anymore. Wanda-Jean was afraid. She wanted to go, to end it, but she didn't want to go like this.

She suddenly wanted to talk to someone. She needed desperately to talk to another human being. She got up. Her legs seemed a very long way away. It was difficult to breathe, and walk. She lurched to the wall and made a badly coordinated grab for the wall phone. At the first attempt she missed. On the second attempt she managed to get a grip on it. She put it to her ear and pressed the button for the operator.

"Operator."

It was a synthetic voice. Wanda-Jean sobbed. "I need to talk to someone."

"I'm sorry, I'm not programmed to process that request. If you require an emergency service, please press three."

"I just want to talk to someone."

"I'm sorry, I'm not programmed to process that request. If you require an emergency service, please press three."

She should call someone, a friend, one of the men in her life. Yeah, right. Call Murray Dorfman, call Bobby Priest, call any of the millions of people who had seen her crawl naked from that tank.

The synthetic voice of the phone was in her ear. "I am breaking the connection. I will report a fault on the line."

The colors around her had become strange. They seemed washed out and dead, as if they were slowly fading to black and white. Wanda-Jean felt terribly tired.

It was very, very hard to stand. Things were fading around her. It was hard to make her thoughts work. She was drifting to an empty warm place. She would be safe there. She wouldn't be.

Wanda-Jean's legs gave way. She slid down the wall

and crumpled in a heap on the floor. Her head lolled onto her shoulder. Her eyes had rolled up into her head.

They didn't find her until three days later.

RALPH TURNED INTO EMPLOYEE ENtrance K as he had done every day, four days a week, for as long as he could remember. The sky was gray and overcast, and the air was sticky. Very soon it would rain, but that probably wouldn't help any. He had spent the night with the woman in the blue coat, so at least he was coming from somewhere different, and that in itself was a novelty. They had gone drinking together after the disturbance outside the Sanyo-Hyatt, and after a couple of hours, she had invited him to go back to her place. It was another cheap-lease as small and as pokey as his. He found it a bit disturbing that the walls were covered with stills from "Wildest Dreams," but he didn't say anything. They made love with the drunken clumsiness of the desperate. It turned out that her name was Nancy, and they made plans to meet later in the week. Ralph wasn't sure how he felt about that. Nancy was a little strange. She had spent too much time alone with her television. He really wasn't sure what he thought about very much at that moment. He had a vicious hangover, and he was still wearing the previous day's clothes. It didn't really matter. No one would notice. He passed his ID card across the scanner and punched himself in. He was actually on time for a change. Nancy lived a lot closer in than he did. He took the elevator down to 5066 section. Sam was already there. Sweeping.

"Morning, Sam."

"Morning, Ralph."

JOHN WILSON HEFFER WAS STILL BILLY the Kid, and his mind was screaming. The dialogue went on and on.

"So I guess there's no way out of this thing."

"Not unless you want to surrender peaceable and come back with me."

"You know I can't do that."

"Then I don't see no way out. We'd better get to it."

Without another word, Billy/Heffer's hand flashed to the Colt, but he wasn't fast enough. The rifle was in Garrett's hand before his own pistol was even clear of its holster. There was a bang, a puff of smoke, and, immediately afterward, a searing, burning pain in his chest that was made doubly bad by the overloaded tactile input. He was thrown back onto the hot, red dirt of the street. The loop of malfunctioning fantasy went around and around, picking him up and knocking him down again, over and over again, and all the time there was the pain of the bullets smashing into his chest. It seemed to have been going on since infinity. The detached part of his mind had curled into a metaphoric fetal ball, praying that madness would come and take away the pain. No one was monitoring, and no one was coming to get him out. All he could hope for was that something would snap and that he would achieve oblivion.

He was suddenly on his feet again.

"So I guess there's no way out of this thing."

"Not unless you want to surrender peaceable and come back with me."

"You know I can't do that."

"Then I don't see no way out. We'd better get to it."

Without another word, Billy/Heffer's hand flashed to his Colt, but he wasn't fast enough. The rifle was in Garrett's hand before his own pistol was even clear of its holster. There was a bang, a puff of smoke, and, immediately afterward, a searing, burning pain in his chest. He was thrown back onto the hot, red dirt of the street.

He was suddenly on his feet again.

"So I guess there's no way out of this thing."

ABOUT THE AUTHOR

In 1979, when the first version of this book was written, Mick Farren was observing punk rock with a grim delight and had become convinced that the world was headed for cultural damnation. In the ensuing ten years, he has seen little reason to revise his opinions.

Introducing...

The Science Fiction Collection

Del Rey has gathered the forces of four of its greatest authors into a thrilling, mind-boggling series that no Science Fiction fan will want to do without!!